MAIL-ORDER DUCHESS

LORDS OF THE ROCKIES
BOOK ONE

MISTY M. BELLER

He tends his flock like a shepherd:
He gathers the lambs in his arms
and carries them close to his heart;
he gently leads those that have young.

Isaiah 40:11 (NIV)

CHAPTER 1

MAY 26, 1869
BALFOUR RANCH, NEAR WALNUT SPRINGS, MONTANA TERRITORY

The quill trembled in Enoch Balfour's hand. As he sat at his desk, the paper before him shifted into the image of William's broken body seared into his mind. He squeezed his eyes shut to fight the memory. The *tick, tick, tick* of the grandfather clock in the great room downstairs echoed through the still house.

He forced his lids open. Forced his focus back on the pen in his hand. He must write this letter, no matter how much it pained him.

> *Dearest Father,*
>
> *It is with a heavy heart that I must share the most grievous news. Our beloved William was—*

His hand shook and a drop of ink splattered across the page. He clenched his jaw, fighting the rising tide of emotion threatening to drown him. He had to be strong, had to fulfill his duty as the eldest now.

But the words wouldn't come.

He pushed to his feet and strode to the window, then gazed out at the snow-capped mountains that had been his refuge these past years. How could he leave this place? Yet what choice did he have?

"William, what am I to do?" His words fogged the glass. "You were meant to lead, not me."

In the reflection, he caught sight of the portrait behind him, above the fireplace—the five Balfour brothers in happier times. William's confident smile twisted a knife in his chest.

Enoch turned away and made himself return to the desk. He sat and took up the quill once more. Finally, the words poured out of him, each one like a drop of his own blood.

> Our beloved William was killed in a tragic accident yesterday, thrown from a horse he was training. His injuries were too severe, and he passed before we could staunch the bleeding. I am undone by grief, as I know you will be.
>
> As I am considered the eldest now, I understand I must uphold the family duties. I will return to England and take my place in parliament as William planned. I ask only for a little more time to settle matters here and bid farewell to the life I have loved.
>
> Your dutiful son,
> Enoch

He pushed the paper away and leaned back in his chair. His

body had little strength left, but his mind...his mind wouldn't rest. If only he'd been there with Will. They could have worked together with the colt. His brother would still be here now.

He stood and stepped to the window. As he stared out, the mountains blurred in front of him. He would have to leave this place. His home. Return to a land that held only hard memories.

Hopefully his father wouldn't force a marriage on him the moment he reached England, the way he'd threatened Will. Father thought Lady Cecilia, the widowed daughter of one of his good friends, the Earl of Canford, would be an excellent match.

After one exchange of letters with the bitter, opinionated woman, Will had chosen to find an American woman—though locating one who met his father's qualifications of genteel upbringing and family ties to England had proven challenging.

No such woman existed out here in the mountain wilderness of the Montana Territory, so Will had started his search with an advertisement in the eastern papers.

Enoch breathed out a sigh. Would he be better off trying the same thing? Will had communicated with a few ladies who responded, but only made a formal offer to one. Thankfully, she'd never sent an agreement. At least, not as far as Enoch knew.

His gut clenched. He'd need to go through Will's correspondence to be certain. One more painful duty.

He had to come to terms with the fact that his life was no longer his own. His dreams, his future, had been changed in one fatal moment.

Like an avalanche sweeping down a mountain, he was powerless to stop the charge. All he could do was face it head-on and pray he would not be found wanting.

Again.

CHAPTER 2

Mandie Beaumont's stomach lurched as the final hymn swelled through the church, the organ notes pounding in her skull. She gripped the edge of the pew, her knuckles white as she fought the rising nausea.

The moment the reverend finished the benediction and people around her began to gather their belongings, she stood and slid out of their row.

"Amanda?" Her mother's voice called behind her. "Where are you going?"

She couldn't stop to answer. Moving made the bile surge up to her throat. She had to reach the powder room before…

Pushing through the door to the ladies' chamber, she barely managed to latch it behind her before everything inside surged out.

She gripped the cool porcelain of the basin as her body trembled with each heave. How much longer would this sickness last?

Two weeks now, and the nausea seemed to be worsening. Maybe she should call for Dr. Wilmont like her housekeeper kept suggesting.

At last, she poured clean water over her hands and wiped her mouth. When she dared straighten, a glance in the mirror showed a worse picture than usual. Her face, pale as parchment. Her eyes, rimmed red, and the shadows underneath, as dark as her hair.

She had to get back before her mother came looking for her. Papa would be off brown-nosing with his constituents, encouraging their votes in the mayoral election this fall. Mama would be doing the same with the ladies, but she would expect Mandie at her side.

She inhaled a deep breath, then cleaned up as best she could.

At last, she took in one more breath for courage and stepped back into the church's main hallway.

Her mother stood near the portrait of the Virgin Mary, engaged in conversation with Mrs. Ashton and her daughter, Louisa, who had married last spring.

As Mandie approached, snippets of their discussion reached her ears.

"...been feeling so poorly, I can barely keep anything down," Louisa was saying, one hand resting on the full skirts covering her middle. "Dr. Wilmont says it's all quite normal in my condition, but I do hope it passes soon."

Mrs. Ashton patted her daughter's arm. "It will, dear. Why, when I was carrying you, I was indisposed for months. But it's all worth it in the end."

Mandie froze. A chilling realization crept through her, dulling Mama's response.

Could she be...with child? The very thought made her ill all over again.

She'd missed her courses last month, but she'd assumed it

was due to the constant stress and fear that Clayton would come for her again.

Perhaps it was more. Perhaps the horrible thing he'd done had left her with more than just nightmares and shame.

Mandie barely felt her mother's hand around her arm, leading her away from the Ashtons with a polite farewell. Her mind reeled with the implications. What would happen if she was found to be with child too long after her husband's death for it to be his?

How could she find out for certain? She couldn't call Dr. Wilmont. He knew every family of their acquaintance. He would tell her parents. And they would…

She couldn't think about what they would do. The scandal. It would ruin her father's chances at the mayoral election, destroying everything he'd worked his entire life to achieve. His dreams.

And her mother…Mandie's heart clenched at the possibility. She'd already been pushing Mandie toward Clayton Beaumont, her deceased husband's brother. No matter that Mandie made it clear she abhorred the man. Would her mother now push harder, knowing Mandie carried his child? Even if she learned the awful way her condition had been forced on her?

Mandie's breath stalled in her lungs. Fear choked her. But she pushed the panic down as her mother guided her through the crowd, smiling and greeting acquaintances. Her mother seemed to have a destination in mind, and Mandie had little strength to protest.

"Clayton, how lovely to see you." Her mother's cheerful greeting made Mandie's chest seize.

Clayton's tall form loomed before them.

No. His dark eyes raked over her in a way that made her skin crawl. The memory of his hands on her, his weight pressing her down, flashed through her mind, and terror clawed at her throat.

She couldn't stand there and pretend everything was fine, not with the truth of what he'd done growing inside her. She had to leave.

She pulled from her mother's grasp and spun away.

Nearly running, she wove between people, her mother's voice calling from behind.

She didn't stop. Not until she reached her carriage, which Mr. Mortimer had thankfully already brought around. He looked down from the driver's bench, and she gave him as much of a smile as she could muster. "Home, please."

Then she jerked the door open and plunged inside. She yanked it shut and collapsed onto the seat, finally letting herself rest.

As the carriage lurched into motion, she leaned her head against the cushioned seat, eyes closed, trying to still the racing of her heart. The jostling of the wheels over cobblestones made her stomach churn again, but she fought it back.

She had to think. To plan.

She couldn't stay in Savannah, that much was certain. Not with the soon-to-be-evident truth of her condition and the scandal that would follow. And certainly not with Clayton prowling around, forcing his suit at every opportunity. She'd told the servants not to allow him entrance to the house. But Clayton used every public opportunity he could find. He'd even won her parents to his cause.

She had to get away from him. But where could she go?

The letter from Mr. Balfour flashed through her mind. His offer for her to come west, to his ranch in the Montana Territory, to meet him and see if they might suit.

She still couldn't believe she'd responded to his advertisement in the *Daily News and Herald,* but the listing had been so unusual. *A rancher of noble birth, seeking a wife gently raised.* And the bit about preference given if she was from England or possessed familial connections living there. The man must be from that country himself. He would likely receive few responses from women who fit his description and were desperate enough to travel to the wild territories for a husband.

She fit the description though. Her grandparents still lived in England on their estate in Kent. Mama had met Papa when he'd visited on his grand tour, and they'd been married before traveling to his home in Savannah.

Was it Providence that led her to Mr. Balfour's advertisement? The thought had prodded her to send him a letter.

At the time, she'd been desperate to find an escape from Clayton's relentless pursuit and her mother's pressure to remarry the moment she was out of mourning.

Mr. Balfour's words had offered a glimmer of hope—a chance at a new life far from the stifling expectations of Savannah society.

Even after mailing the letter, she'd not truly believed anything would come of it.

But his response had been prompt and gentlemanly, expressing his sincere desire to make her acquaintance and explore the possibility of a match. He'd made it clear she would be under no obligation, that she could return home if she found his ranch in the west unsuitable.

That option sounded far more promising than staying in Savannah. Here, so close to Clayton's clutches. Yet could she trust this stranger to be any better? At least there, she would have choices.

God, is this the right step?

She waited, listening, searching for an internal tug.

Nothing came, but something in her spirit felt a little quieter. Not quite at peace but…settled with the decision.

As soon as she reached her townhouse, Mandie hurried inside, ignoring the concerned looks from the servants. She made her way up the sweeping staircase to her room and latched the door behind her.

With shaking hands, she pulled out the letter from Mr. Balfour and read it again, though she'd nearly memorized every word. His descriptions of the vast mountains and untamed wilderness called to a part of her soul she hadn't known existed. A place where she could start anew, free from the shame and scandal that would surely follow if she stayed.

A new thought slipped in. When he found out about the baby, would he turn her away? She inhaled another deep breath and straightened her shoulders. If he did, she could simply buy a home there and settle on her own. She had more than enough money from her late husband's businesses to live on, and she would be free from Clayton's pressures.

She moved to her writing desk and pulled out a sheet of paper. But as she dipped the pen in the inkwell, she hesitated. If she sent a letter, it would likely reach him at the same time she did.

A telegram would be faster. She would send it today and make preparations to depart on a morning train. Her maid, Abigail, would help her pack in secret. She could trust her to keep this confidence. Abigail had become a good friend these past few years.

Mandie took a deep breath and began to write, choosing her words carefully to fit the telegram's brevity.

MR. WILLIAM BALFOUR STOP ACCEPT YOUR OFFER STOP DEPARTING SAVANNAH NEXT TRAIN STOP WILL WIRE UPON ARRIVAL IN ST LOUIS STOP RESPECTFULLY AMANDA BEAUMONT FULL STOP

As she read over the words, her heart pounded even harder. This was madness, leaving everything she'd ever known for a strange man in an even stranger land. But also…exhilarating.

What would he be like? Rugged? Hard-edged? His letter made him sound kind.

Her Nicholas had been kind, though distant. If she could find another such man, she'd be thankful.

Whatever this Montana rancher was like, she would learn the truth soon enough.

CHAPTER 3

August 29, 1869

Balfour Ranch, near Walnut Springs, Montana Territory

Sweat trickled down Enoch's neck as he led the defiant young mare to the larger corral so she could run with the other horses in training. Her ears flicked back in muted rebellion, even after he'd removed the saddle. She'd been the hardest of the three he rode today.

He patted the horse's damp shoulder. "Good girl. That's enough for today." Then he opened the gate and released her to trot as far away from him as she could manage in the small pasture.

As he watched her go, he shook his head. She'd come around in time, but it would take patience and consistency. Two things in short supply these days.

He released a heavy sigh as he hung the rope on a post. Already three months had passed, yet still, every thought reminded him of Will.

The sun hung low over the western peaks, painting the sky in shades of fire that echoed the turmoil in his chest. He should head inside, clean up for the evening meal. Mrs. Wang liked them all to be punctual.

Exhaustion pressed heavy as he turned to the house. The big log structure had been home for most of his life, ever since they fled England when he was six years old to escape the schemes of his father's cousin, Reginald. That villain had proved he'd do anything to take over Father's title as the Duke of Clarence.

Reginald had first tried to discredit them by attacking their mother's Scottish heritage and Catholic loyalties, claiming they made her—and by extension, the boys—unfit heirs in the eyes of the Church of England. When that didn't work, he'd had Will kidnapped. Held him for a day before Father's men tracked the lad down and brought him home.

That ordeal had been the breaking point, driving Father to send their mother, him, and his brothers to Montana with the Wangs, far from Reginald's reach. They'd had this home built as a temporary refuge, but after Mother's death two years later, Father's grief had kept him from sending for their return to England. By the time he finally raised the notion, Enoch and all four of his brothers loved this wild country far more than they'd ever appreciated the country of their birth.

Now, warm lamplight already spilled from the windows of the kitchen and dining room. He would miss this place. Would he ever get to return?

The weight pressed harder on his chest. What did he do so wrong that God would only strip away the people he loved? First his mother. Then Charlotte, the woman he'd been betrothed to marry. And her parents—parents who had felt more like his than the Duke of Clarence, who lived so far away. Then Mr. Wang, who'd been more like an uncle than a manservant to them all these years in the Montana.

And now William. On top of that, he would have to step into William's role and leave these mountains that had become part of his soul.

He trudged up the porch steps with the last of his energy and wiped his boots on the braided rug before opening the door to step into the great room.

Aromas of onion, sage, and roasting meat wafted from the kitchen—rabbit stew, most like. Mrs. Wang had a knack for making even the humblest fare fit for a king.

As Enoch turned into the dining room, Robert looked up from setting a steaming pan of cornbread on the table. Whether managing the ranch's records or helping Mrs. Wang with one of the many tasks around the ranch, he applied the same precision to every task.

His brother motioned toward the dining room. "James and Thomas aren't back from town yet, but Mrs. Wang doesn't want the food to get cold."

Enoch nodded. No surprise there.

Their housekeeper would keep the rest warm for when his other brothers returned, ensuring each of them had a hot meal no matter how late they rode in. She always went out of her way to make them feel cared for.

"I'll wash up." He headed to the small closet where Mr. Wang had once installed a pump. The man had been talented enough to build anything, with a mind that understood the laws of physics as well as Galileo. These last four years had been hard without him, and not just because of his skill with constructing things.

As he scrubbed the dirt and sweat from his hands and face, the cool water brought a welcome respite from the lingering heat and the turmoil in his mind. He stared at his reflection in the small mirror above the basin. The man looking back at him appeared older, wearier than he should. Haggard even.

He dried his face and hands on the towel, then straightened his shoulders and walked back to the dining room. Robert had finished setting the table, and Mrs. Wang carried in a large tureen of steaming stew. The savory scent made his stomach rumble, the apple and cheese he'd eaten at midday long gone.

"Smells delicious." He managed a smile for the woman who had been a constant, comforting presence in their lives for as long as he could remember.

She smiled back, the creases in her weathered face nearly covering her almond-shaped eyes. "You sit and eat now, Lord Enoch. You work too hard."

She'd always insisted on using their titles, even as lads. She was the only one left in the area who even knew their connection to the peerage, and tucked away as they were, an hour and a half from the closest small town of Walnut Springs, he'd long since made peace with allowing her this freedom. In truth, anything Mrs. Wang wanted, he'd march through fire to get her.

He took his seat beside Robert, with Mrs. Wang at the end of the table nearest the kitchen. William's seat at the head remained empty.

And it would stay that way. No one could fill his brother's place.

Enoch might be considered the eldest now, but he would take none of the liberties the position granted. Only the duties he couldn't avoid.

Robert cleared his throat. "Shall we pray?" At Enoch's nod, he bowed his head. "Lord, we thank you for this bounty and for the hands that prepared it. We ask your blessings on our family, both here and far away. May you guide and protect us all. Amen."

As Enoch echoed his own, "Amen," the front door banged open, announcing the arrival of James and Thomas. His younger brothers' boisterous voices filled the house as they stomped into the dining room.

James, with his golden-brown hair tousled from the ride and his green eyes sparkling with his usual charm, entered with a ready smile that made him look younger than his twenty-four years. He tossed his hat on the tree by the door. "Sorry we're late. Got caught up talking to Timmons."

Thomas, his dark hair in need of a trim and his eyes holding a mischievous look that belied his keen observation, held out a small envelope to Enoch. "This came for you. Looks like it's from England."

Enoch took the telegram, his stomach twisted. Father must have received his letter about William.

Mrs. Wang *tsked* at the other two. "You go wash up now. The meal is getting cold."

As both men tromped to the wash closet, Enoch gripped the paper, but didn't unfold it. Should he wait until after the meal, when he could read the note alone?

But Robert and Mrs. Wang watched him, eagerness in their gazes.

With an inward sigh, Enoch slid his thumb beneath the flap and unfolded the paper. He scanned the short message.

DEAREST ENOCH STOP RECEIVED LETTER DEEPEST GRIEF STOP MARRIAGE MORE IMPORTANT THAN PARLIAMENT STOP EITHER STAY AND WAIT FOR WILLIAMS BRIDE OR LADY CECILIA AWAITS IN ENGLAND FULL STOP

He stared at the words, unable to will them into something more palatable. A wife. The notion settled like a stone in his gut. His father would require it already.

Enoch had spent the past months steeling himself for the journey to England, for the life of a duke-in-training, but now marriage too? He'd not been able to bring himself to consider that as a real possibility.

Not since Charlotte. The old pain twisted in his chest. He'd determined not to risk loving again. The pain wasn't worth any pleasure that might come of an attachment.

Mrs. Wang and Robert exchanged a glance, no doubt noting the tension in his posture. He tried to school his features, but frustration simmered too close to the surface.

James and Thomas returned, their earlier joviality subdued for once. Maybe they sensed the shift in the room. They took their seats, glancing between Enoch and the telegram.

"Well?" James raised an eyebrow. "What news from the motherland?" His voice came a touch too casual. They'd probably read the telegram when they picked it up.

He didn't have the energy to call them out though.

He tossed the paper on the table, as if physical distance could lessen its impact. "Father wants me to stay here until the bride William sent for arrives." The words fell like stones, heavy and immovable. They'd received a wire from her accepting Will's offer and saying she'd send a note when she arrived in St. Louis. "Unfortunately, I've already sent her a telegram not to come." Once she received his note in St. Louey, she'd head back to where she came from.

James eyed him. "You could always send another, inviting her once more. Or place the advertisement again."

Thomas reached for the telegram, skimming the contents. "I think it's a capital suggestion. About time you settled down."

Robert nodded. "A wife could be good for you. And you know Father won't rest until you secure an heir."

Enoch's jaw locked. Good for him? What did Robert know of it? He'd never lost the woman he loved, never felt the ache of a shattered heart. Robert lived in the safe, orderly world of his ledgers and figures.

Thomas jumped in with his usual easy charm. "Come now, it might not be so bad. Think of it as an adventure. A mystery bride, sent to tame the wild Montana bachelor."

Enoch shot him a dark look. "This isn't one of your dime novels. This is my life." They didn't understand the gravity of what was being asked of him. The very idea of marriage tied his insides in knots.

He pushed back from the table, the screech of wood loud. "Forgive me, Mrs. Wang. I fear I've lost my appetite."

Her dark eyes held sympathy and concern, but she merely nodded. "I'll keep it warm for you."

He inclined his head in gratitude, then strode toward the front door, snatching his hat as he passed the rack. The walls closed in, suffocating him. He needed air. Space to think.

Outside, the mountain air had already cooled. He gulped it in, anything to clear his head. The sun hung low over the snow-capped peaks around them, painting the sky in streaks of orange and pink. This sight usually brought him peace, but now it only stirred a restless agitation in his blood.

He needed to move, to do something physical to quiet the clamor in his mind.

He headed toward the barn, his boots scuffing on the hard-packed earth. He'd check the stock in the east pasture, make sure they were settled for the night. It would give him time to pull himself back together.

As he walked, he couldn't help sending a question upward. *Haven't I already dealt with enough death and disappointment?* Nothing he'd planned was coming to pass. Why would this marriage be different?

But no booming voice answered. Not even a niggle in his mind.

His gelding, Leif, had already worked hard that day, so he saddled Will's mare. She needed exercise.

As he swung up into the seat and turned his mount toward the upper pasture, he could almost believe he was riding away from the expectations, the suffocating weight of duty.

But even as the ranch house receded behind him, the telegram burned in his mind, an inescapable reminder of the choice that had been made for him.

Another choice. One he would have to find a way to bear, no matter the cost to his mind and heart.

CHAPTER 4

andie gripped Mr. Balfour's letter tighter. The paper crinkled beneath her gloved fingers as she stepped off the steamship's gangplank onto the rough wooden dock.

She'd made it. Finally.

The grueling two-month trip had left her exhausted. Now, relief and panic warred for control of her shaking limbs. Was she really doing this? Marrying a stranger in a strange land?

She wouldn't turn back now. She willed herself to move forward.

Fort Benton bustled ahead—a mass of men and mud. Workers shouted as they loaded and unloaded the three steamships lining the dock. Wagons clattered by on the road that ran along the riverfront. And the smells… The two she could pick out were the tangy smell of livestock and the rich scent of wood smoke, but so many other odors laced together to flood her senses.

Men streamed past her like water around one of the many islands in the middle of the Missouri River. She'd better get out of the way before she was knocked to the ground.

The first order of business had to be finding the telegraph office. She hadn't received a telegram in St. Louis as she'd expected, so Mr. Balfour would have left instructions in this town, most likely, since it was the final steamboat stop on the journey. She'd already had her trunks sent on to the hotel, but she needed to take care of this matter before settling in. She had to know what her next step should be.

Mandie wove through the throng of people, off the dock, and onto the muddy street. She gathered her skirts and stepped around the puddles and piles of horse droppings, making her way toward the rough wooden buildings that lined the opposite side of the street.

She must seem so out of place amidst the rough-hewn men in their dusty work clothes. And the beards...nearly every one of these fellows wore full, untrimmed beards that flowed down to their chests. The only men who didn't were the dark-haired natives. She'd known she would see Indians in the west, but she'd not expected them to be in town, strolling around like they had as much business to accomplish here as the white men.

No one she passed regarded the natives with concern, so she did her best not to do so either.

In truth, it was *her* they gawked at.

She'd heard there weren't many women in the west, but she'd not expected to be such a novelty. Did her well-tailored traveling dress mark her as an outsider?

Perhaps she should have changed into one of her plainer gowns before disembarking from the ship. She had brought them, anticipating the journey would be dirty and challenging. The week on the train from Savannah to St. Louis *had* been so. But stepping aboard the *Lacon* steamboat had been like entering a fine hotel, complete with richly furnished parlors and small but well-appointed staterooms.

Now this Fort Benton place looked like she'd fully reached the frontier. Once she found lodging, she could change into a less-conspicuous dress. But first, she had to learn what accommodations Mr. Balfour had made for the remainder of her journey. And she couldn't let a few bold gazes delay her.

As she walked, she kept her chin lifted and her shoulders back. A bit of poise and grace could overcome any setback.

Skimming the storefronts, she scanned the hand-painted signs for any indication of a telegraph office. She almost missed the small plaque in the window of a mercantile that said "U.S. Post and Telegraph Office."

At the doorway, she paused to gather herself and smooth down the front of her skirt. No sense charging in like a blustering, unmannerly wind.

Inside, shelves and tables filled the small building, with wares piled on every surface—except a counter in one corner. She stepped in that direction.

An older man met her there, one who looked a little more like a shopkeeper than all those she'd seen on the street. "Mail or telegram?" His tone was polite, but his raised eyebrow suggested he found her presence unusual.

She offered a confident smile. "I'm hoping there might be a message waiting for me. From a Mr. William Balfour."

"And your name is?"

Of course he would need that. "Mrs. Beaumont."

The man frowned as he flipped through a stack of papers on the counter. "Nothing here for a Mrs. Beaumont." He looked up at her, his expression apologetic. "When were you expecting this message?"

Mandie's chest tightened, but she maintained her composure. "I had hoped it would arrive before I did. Mr. Balfour was supposed to send instructions for the remainder of my journey to his ranch near Walnut Springs."

"Well, now, that's not unusual. Sometimes the telegraph lines are down to the smaller towns out in the territory. If he sent something, it might still be on its way."

She nodded, trying to hide her disappointment. "I see." What now? Should she wait until the telegram came through? "How long do repairs usually take?"

He tipped his head, his expression thoughtful. "Hard to say. Sometimes a week, sometimes months if the line goes down far from town."

Months? She couldn't possibly wait here that long.

Disappointment fought with determination in her chest. She'd come so far already. She could make her own travel arrangements for the last stretch. She certainly couldn't wait here for months, facing an uncertain future.

She forced a pleasant smile. "Thank you. Can you recommend how I might arrange passage to Walnut Springs?"

The clerk tapped a finger on the counter as his gaze turned thoughtful. "I know the name, but I can't recall exactly where that is. You might try the livery down the way. They'll know best. Over one street and to the left." He motioned the direction she needed to go.

She thanked the man and stepped back into the sunlit street. His directions had been vague, but they took her close enough to hear the clanging of metal on metal. A sign halfway down the block proclaimed, "Livery and Blacksmith."

Three rowdy men outside the rough-hewn building fell silent at her approach. They scanned her up and down, whispering amongst themselves. Though her cheeks scalded, she did her best to project an air of belonging as she walked, despite the lingering stares following her progress.

The livery doors stood open, and she stepped through to escape the leering, but paused inside to let her eyes adjust from the bright sun.

The scent of hay and horses filled her nose. The hammering ceased and a burly man with wild red hair looked up from his work at the forge. He set down his tools and wiped his hands on his leather apron.

"Help ye, lass?" His Irish accent gave a lilt to his words, but not enough to make him hard to understand.

She stepped farther into the space, toward the flickering light from the forge. "I'm hoping you can, sir. I need passage to Walnut Springs. I was told you might be able to assist me."

The man's thick brows lifted in surprise. "Walnut Springs, ye tell me? T'at be a fair journey from here, 'specially for a lady traveling alone. Whereabouts are ye headed, if I may ask?"

She hesitated only a moment before replying. "I'm to meet Mr. William Balfour there."

"Ah, t'e Balfour Ranch." He nodded, his expression thoughtful. "I know it. Up in the high country, so it is. Nestled in a pretty valley. Good grazing land, from what I hear."

His familiarity with the location eased some of the tension in her shoulders. At least she was on the right track. "That's the one. I had hoped Mr. Balfour would have sent word on how to complete my journey, but it seems his message has been delayed."

"Not unusual, t'at." His beard tugged up at the corners, and his eyes softened. "T'e telegraph lines are a mite unpredictable in these parts. But no matter. If it's Walnut Springs ye be wanting, I could have an answer for ye."

Mandie's heart leapt. "I would be most grateful for any assistance."

The man nodded toward the open doors at the back of the livery. "I've a fellow out t'ere now, loading up a wagon for a journey in t'at direction. Name's Two Stones, and he's traveling with his new wife. He's a native, but t'ere's none more capable, and none more trustworthy either. If he's willing, he could see ye there safe, so he could."

Mandie followed his gaze to the bright yard behind the stable. A tall figure moved around a wagon, securing a cover over the contents. His raven-black hair shone in the sunlight like the natives she'd passed in the street. He wore a loose cotton shirt and trousers like many of the white men though.

How could she trust a stranger? Or rather, two strangers, with his wife along. And natives especially. The stories she'd heard on the steamboat ride...

She turned back to the livery owner, a nervous flutter in her stomach. "Is there not a stagecoach or other form of public passage?"

He offered a grim smile. "Sorry, lass. The last stage driver headed east before winter hit, an' we've not had another step up since t'en. Ye could rent a horse or wagon and team. Else ride along with someone goin' that direction." He hesitated. "I can tell you if I were choosin' who I'd trust to drive me there, Two Stones would be top of my list."

A wagon. And a strange man and woman. Did she dare? What choice did she have?

"How long will the trip take?"

He tipped his head. "I don't travel it often, but I'd say a week an' a half or so. Dependin' on t'e weather."

A week and a half. With strangers.

She took in a steadying breath to quell the panic rising in her chest. "You said his wife would travel with us?"

Another woman, even a native woman, would make the situation more palatable. Did either of them speak English?

The blacksmith turned and motioned for her to follow. "Let's go get the particulars from him."

Part of her wanted to plant her feet and object. This was happening too quickly. She needed to decide if she even wanted to ride with strangers before she met him.

But she followed the livery owner, past rows of stalls on either side. A few horses nickered greetings as they passed, and the man returned soft words to each, though he kept walking.

When they stepped into the yard, the warm, relaxing touch of sun eased her tension, at least a little.

Two Stones paused in his work and turned to regard them. The flat line of his lips made his expression unreadable.

Up close, he was even taller than she'd first thought, with broad shoulders that spoke of much physical labor. His dark eyes studied her as though he could see right through her carefully composed facade to her apprehension beneath.

The livery owner spoke first. "Two Stones, this is Mrs. Beaumont. She's needing passage to Walnut Springs, and mayhap on to t'e Balfour Ranch. Since ye and yer missus are headed that direction, I told her ye might be able to see her there safely."

Two Stones studied her another long moment. She met his gaze as steadily as she could, doing her best to project an air of quiet confidence despite the fluttering in her middle.

"I have two trunks, and I'm happy to pay." She added, "For your trouble and any provisions needed for the journey."

At last, Two Stones gave a single nod, his expression still unreadable. "We have room. You are welcome with us. The journey will be long."

Us. She sighed at the term. "Thank you. I am prepared to do what I must." She hesitated, then added, "Your wife...will be traveling with us as well?"

He gave another nod, and a glimmer of a smile flashed in his eyes.

Relief eased through her. "I look forward to meeting her. When do you plan to depart?"

"First light tomorrow. We can meet here."

Tomorrow. So soon. But also, not soon enough.

"Thank you." She took a step back and glanced at the livery owner. "Thank you both for your assistance."

Now if she could find her way to the hotel, she could organize her thoughts and change into a dress more fitting for this next step in her new life.

CHAPTER 5

Mandie's entire body ached from so many days of jostling on this wagon's unforgiving seat. Yet, according to Two Stones, they would finally reach Walnut Springs by the end of today. Thank the Father above.

The quiet man had proven to be every bit as capable and trustworthy as the livery owner promised. And his wife, Heidi, who sat beside Mandie on the wagon bench, had become a wonderful new friend—and nothing at all like Mandie expected.

She was a white woman, and apparently Heidi and Two Stones had only been married last December, not long after Heidi came west to join her father in one of the mining towns. Her father passed away soon after her arrival, but with his final breaths, he'd begged Two Stones to marry his daughter—a strong recommendation for the man's character.

Their marriage might have started out as a union born from hard circumstances, but anyone who saw the pair together could easily see the love flowing between them. Two Stones was gentle with her, giving her such deference. And he truly seemed to enjoy her presence. Though reading his thoughts and emotions could still be a challenge because of his stony expressions.

Soon Mandie would say farewell to these two new friends.

Yet how wonderful would it be to finally reach the town of Walnut Springs, where she would have a proper bed and a real privy and bathtub. Layers of grime caked her, pasted on through many hours of sweat.

Even now, her mind could conjure the exquisite feel of sinking into a tub of steaming water, the heat soothing her travel-weary muscles. Lavender-scented soap would wash away the grime of the frontier, leaving her skin soft and refreshed. She'd take her time combing out the tangles in her long brown hair until it gleamed. Then she would put on a fresh dress. Something wonderfully clean.

After all that, when she looked and felt like herself again, she could send a message to Mr. Balfour to let him know she'd arrived.

Two Stones had said they could take a different trail directly to the Balfour ranch and reach it at about the same time as they would the town, but she'd rather take time to make herself presentable before meeting the man she might marry.

Despite the discomfort of the journey, she couldn't deny the raw beauty of this majestic land. Peaks rose around them in every direction, a few still wearing snow-capped crowns that glinted in the midday sun. This was a world apart from the genteel society she'd left behind in Savannah, where every moment was dictated by the expectations of others.

Beside her, Heidi shifted on the seat. "Looks like the rain will be here soon."

Heidi extracted her hand from the crook of her husband's arm and turned to reach into the wagon bed behind them. "We'll be wanting these oilcloths again for shelter."

Mandie took one of the coverings, but she would wait until the first drops fell before she opened it to hold over her head.

They'd been driving uphill for nearly an hour now, and the tall pines on either side had changed to shorter scrubby trees and boulders.

As the wagon swayed, she shifted her hand to rest on her middle. Now that her sickness had lessened, she'd started to relish cradling the babe like this. It felt like a connection—an acknowledgement—of the life growing inside her.

What would this child think of her? Would the child hate her for how he or she came to be? Her fingers tightened against the fabric of her dress, as if she could shield the babe from the truth. She hadn't chosen this—not the widowhood, not the attack, not the man who'd sired her babe.

Her eyes stung, but she blinked the tears away. *I didn't ask for you. But you're mine now, little one. I'll be the very best mother I can.*

She glanced over the side of the mountain they climbed. The landscape stretched beyond her vision, wild and untamed—a land of second chances, or so the stories claimed. Out here, she could start fresh.

She would meet Mr. Balfour, but take her time choosing whether to marry him or start a life alone with her child. She had plenty of finances to make that work.

She and the babe only needed a simple life—a little house with a cozy kitchen and hearth, a garden blooming in the spring, a child laughing in the yard.

And if she chose Mr. Balfour…what then? That picture came far less clear.

A ranch house? With pastures of cattle and horses? What if, when he learned about the baby, Mr. Balfour turned her away? What if he didn't want the scandal? The burden of an unexpected baby? What then?

She drew in a steadying breath, then released it.

She couldn't let fear win. She had choices in her life. And God wouldn't bring her here just to abandon her. She lifted her eyes to the sky, blue and boundless, and let the thought settle over her like a prayer. *You have a plan here, Lord. Don't you?*

Peace settled in her spirit, especially as her gaze caught on a hawk soaring over the trees. Maybe she didn't have answers yet, but she had the God who created this majesty. And He'd promised to work this situation for her good. That would be enough.

A few minutes later, the first drops landed on her face. She and Heidi pulled open their oilcloths.

Those first patters moved quickly into heavy sheets, and the wind picked up, whipping the covering around Mandie's face. She gripped tighter, trying to maintain her balance against the buffeting torrent.

Two Stones guided the wagon to the side of the road and pulled the horses to a halt. As he set the brake, a flash of lightning split the sky, sending her heart lurching. Thunder rumbled close behind.

He jumped to the ground and turned to help Heidi descend. Mandie climbed down on her side, gripping the wagon to keep from slipping on the wet step. Her damp skirts didn't help matters, tangling around her legs. The oilcloth did little to keep the rain from soaking through her clothes.

"Come on this side, Mandie," Heidi shouted to be heard over the downpour as she motioned Mandie around the wagon.

When she joined the others, they huddled beside the rig, using the boulders and the wagon itself as a windbreak.

The storm raged on, the wind howling through the trees and driving the rain in stinging sheets against their faces.

Mandie leaned closer to Heidi and said a silent prayer of thanks for the woman's presence in the face of nature's fury. Two Stones had positioned himself on Heidi's other side, where he would receive the brunt of the wind's force.

She had no idea how much time passed—maybe half an

hour? Finally, the thunder's rumble faded into the distance, and the rain slowed to a drizzle.

Mandie lifted her head, blinking away the water that clung to her lashes. The world around them looked so different, the once-dusty trail now a muddy ribbon winding down the slope.

"I guess it's over." Heidi stood and shook out her oilcloth before draping it over her arm. "We should be on our way if we hope to reach town by nightfall."

Mandie nodded, but as she rose, a pressing need made itself known. "I'd best find a private spot first, if you don't mind." Her cheeks warmed at the admission, but after so many days on the trail together, they'd all become accustomed to the realities of travel.

"Of course." Heidi gave an understanding smile. "We'll wait here."

Mandie picked her way up the muddy slope toward a patch of boulders and small trees. They should hide her from view of the wagon.

After finishing her task, she stepped back onto the wet stones to cross to the wagon.

Her foot slipped on the slick surface, sliding out from underneath her. She flailed her arms for balance, grabbing for a rock or branch—anything. But found only air.

Her rear landed on a stone at the same time her head thunked against a larger boulder behind her. Pain exploded through her skull.

Darkness swam at the edges of her vision.

The babe.

She couldn't let her child be hurt. She fought to stay conscious, terror gripping her heart. But she could do nothing to stop her world from going black.

CHAPTER 6

*E*noch rode into the ranch yard as the sun dipped behind the mountains, casting long shadows across the valley. His muscles ached from a day spent tending cattle in the farthest pastures, and dust clung to his clothes and skin, gritty against the dried sweat.

The familiar scent of woodsmoke drifted from the cookstove chimney, curling into the evening air.

But something felt off.

His gelding nickered, and a horse in the barn answered. Did they have a visitor?

The thought stirred a quiet warning he couldn't shake.

Before he could swing down from his saddle, the front door opened and James and Thomas emerged from the house. He couldn't read their expressions, but something was up.

"You're back." James's voice sounded tight. "You'll never guess."

"What's wrong?" Enoch dismounted, his boots hitting the ground with a thud that echoed in his bones. He straightened, brushing a hand across his dust-streaked trousers.

Thomas glanced at James, hesitating, then met Enoch's gaze.

"William's bride arrived today. Two Stones and his new wife brought her. But the woman's injured—took a fall on her way here."

The words hit Enoch like a punch to the gut. *William's bride.* Had she not received the telegram then?

Dread rose in his throat, bitter and thick, but he swallowed it down. "Is she all right?"

"She's resting now." James shifted his weight. "Mrs. Wang is with her. But she's confused—doesn't remember much about why she's here."

Enoch frowned. That didn't bode well. Was she usually of a fragile mind? "Take me to her."

He tied his horse at the porch, then followed his brothers up the stairs and in the door. The scent of something savory wrapped around him like a blanket, though it did nothing to ease the tension coiling in his gut. Beneath the welcome smells lingered something else, a heaviness that made his pulse quicken.

His brothers started down the hallway, and a new uneasiness crept through him. The only bed chambers that direction were his room and William's. Had they placed her in…?

Sure enough, James and Thomas stopped in front of their eldest brother's room, moving to one side of the doorway so he could enter.

He halted in the opening. Mrs. Wang sat in a chair beside the bed holding a damp cloth.

The figure in the bed…blankets covered all but her pale cheek and dark hair. Her face turned away from him, so he couldn't make out many features. But just the bit he could see looked far too dainty to survive in the wilderness.

Mrs. Wang rose and came to meet him. "She's been drifting in and out of sleep." She kept her voice hushed. "The poor dear is exhausted and confused."

Enoch's jaw tightened. He didn't want to think of this

stranger as a *poor dear.* Not when her presence might upend his world.

He stepped closer to the bed where he could study the woman's face. High cheekbones, a delicate nose, lips that looked soft, even in sleep. She was lovely, he had to admit. But beauty alone wouldn't be enough out here.

He turned back to take in Mrs. Wang and his brothers, keeping his voice low. "Have you told her about William?"

James shook his head. "She didn't seem to know what she was doing here. When we mentioned his name, she acted like she'd never heard it."

Mrs. Wang touched his arm. "She needs rest now. There will be time to sort everything later."

He nodded. He could view this as a reprieve. He had all night to stew on what to do with her.

He raised his brows at Mrs. Wang. "James said Two Stones brought her?" He'd met the man several times in town. Sold him a donkey once. The kind of fellow you could tell was trustworthy after just a short conversation.

Mrs. Wang slipped her hand around his waist, guiding him toward the door. "I showed him and his new bride to the extra chamber upstairs. They'll be down to eat in a quarter hour, so you'd best be cleaned up and ready. Robert is tending the meat pies for me."

He let her lead him into the hallway, resting his arm around her shoulders. Mrs. Wang was a good two heads shorter than him, but she felt so much like a mother. And yet his own mother had been tall and fine-boned with no extra curves that often came as women aged. The exact opposite of Mrs. Wang's shape.

He'd only been eight when Mother passed from a lingering fever, so he didn't remember as much about her as he wished. But Mrs. Wang had been a quiet stand-in. A steady presence through all the years they'd grown up in these mountains.

When they reached the main room, she gave his waist a final

squeeze, then pulled back. "You boys see that you're respectable and prompt for dinner. I'm going to sit with Mrs. Beaumont."

Mrs. Beaumont. The name sounded like she would be older, perhaps frumpy or at least wizened. Not this young, angelic creature.

Will had told them the woman had been widowed long enough to be out of mourning, though she was still young. Yet that fact hadn't formed into any kind of picture in Enoch's mind.

As his brothers left to obey their orders, Enoch headed out to put his horse away. A quarter hour didn't leave him time to linger in the barn as he'd like to—far from the people who'd invaded their privacy.

But he was the man of the house now. He no longer had the liberty to hide away when he wasn't ready to face the changes others forced on him.

When the time came for the evening meal, he stood behind his chair at the dining table and waited for Heidi to sit. She'd insisted they call her by her given name. She wasn't at all what he'd expected in Two Stones's wife, but a sort of connection hummed between the pair, strong enough even he could see it. The little glances they slid each other. The way Heidi's cheeks pinkened when she met her husband's gaze. Two Stones's eyes were usually hard to read, but when he looked at his wife, his admiration shimmered without restraint.

Would he and Charlotte have had such an affection if…if her life hadn't been cut so very short?

He pushed aside the pain that twisted in his chest and sat when the other men did.

Robert cleared his throat, his gaze darting to their visitors. "Shall we say a blessing?"

Heidi graced him with a smile as she and Two Stones bowed their heads. Enoch did the same, but keeping his mind on his brother's prayer proved more than he could manage.

At last, they'd all filled their plates and began eating, which meant he could ask questions. He fixed his gaze on Two Stones. "Tell me about the woman you brought. How did she come to travel with you?"

Two Stones regarded him. "We met her in Fort Benton. Irish brought her to me for passage to Walnut Springs. She said she was to meet William Balfour there."

Heidi leaned forward. "She was surprised William hadn't sent word or arranged for her travel from Fort Benton. But she wouldn't turn back—said she'd get here on her own if she had to."

The knot in his gut twisted tighter. "She never got the telegram I sent about William's death." He'd not really thought about it from the woman's perspective. She'd crossed the country alone, expecting a husband to greet her at her destination. A husband who could never be.

Enoch should have tried harder to reach her. Should have done more than send a single telegram.

And now, she was here, bruised and broken, lying in William's bed with no idea of the truth.

He forced his voice to keep steady, though it rasped against the dryness in his throat. "What happened to her on the way?"

Two Stones chewed a bite of meat pie, his dark eyes studying Enoch. "We stopped to wait out a thunderstorm. After the rain, she slipped on a rock. Hit her head."

Heidi's soft voice chimed in. "She has several bruises and a gash near the base of her skull. It took a minute for her to wake up, but then her words seemed addled. Before the rain, she asked us to take her to Walnut Springs so she could have time to rest before your brother came for her, but given the situation, we decided it might be best to bring her straight to your ranch so she wouldn't need to be moved again."

Enoch's chest tightened, a sharp pang he couldn't name. Sympathy, maybe. He knew the kind of headache she must be suffering. Perhaps a bit of admiration stirred somewhere in him too. She didn't belong here. And yet, she'd come anyway. Alone. That took a kind of courage. Foolishness too, which wouldn't do her any favors out here.

Maybe this first injury was a harbinger of what would come.

He pushed a piece of crust around his plate. "She could've died from a fall like that."

Two Stones nodded, his gaze flicking to Heidi with a flash of protectiveness. "We kept her safe. Brought her straight here once we patched her up."

Enoch clenched his jaw. *Safe.* She might be safe now, but for how long?

This territory didn't care about grit or good intentions—it chewed up the strong and the weak alike. He'd seen it too many times—homesteaders broken by blizzards, travelers lost to rivers or bears.

Charlotte's face flashed again—her bright smile dimmed forever by the storm that took her and her parents. He should've protected her.

Should've protected William, too. Should have been there in case that horse gave him trouble.

And now Mrs. Beaumont, another life entrusted to his care. Another life he might very well fail to protect.

James's voice cut through the haze of his thoughts. "What's your plan now, Enoch? Will you marry her as Father asked?"

The question hung heavy, suffocating.

Marry.

Maybe that was his duty. Marry her in William's place, give her a home, a name. It was the honorable thing, especially with her injured and stranded so far from her home. Would she want to live in England? Will must have told her he and his new wife would be moving there.

The thought of tying himself to a stranger, of risking his heart again, made his skin crawl. He didn't want this.

Maybe marrying her didn't have to mean love. Maybe it could just be a roof over her head, a name to keep her safe. A partnership. The idea felt thin, brittle even, but it was something he could hold onto.

Except….he had to produce an heir. A son to carry on the title. His father wouldn't rest until Enoch accomplished his duty. Could he keep his heart out of fathering a child?

James still waited for an answer, so he forced the words out. "I'll talk to her when she's stronger. I'll see if she wants to stay. To…marry me, since William can't."

Thomas leaned forward, his eyes narrowing. "And if she says no?"

Enoch stared past him, out the window, where the last streaks of daylight bled into the mountains. "Then I'll get her back to Savannah. Or wherever she wants to go. She won't be left with nothing."

The table went quiet, the clink of forks the only sound. He felt their eyes on him—Robert's steady gaze, James's skepticism, Thomas's smirk, Heidi's gentle pity. Even Two Stones's perceptive stare.

Not only would he have to eventually leave this home he loved and go to England—the land he hadn't seen since he was six years old—now he would have to take a wife.

Duty had him cornered, and there was no running from it. Not this time.

The remainder of dinner blurred past, the talk turning to safer things—the cattle, the weather, Two Stones's plans for the winter.

When the meal ended and the others drifted off—Two Stones and Heidi upstairs, his brothers to their chores—Enoch stepped outside. The night air hit him like a slap—chilly, cutting through the fog in his head.

He tilted his face to the sky, where stars burned bright and indifferent, scattered across the expanse like spilled salt. They dwarfed him, made him feel small, a speck in a world too big to care about his struggles.

Was his father staring up at these same stars, somewhere across the Atlantic? That world had always seemed so far away. He barely had any memories of England. And yet he was expected to call it home.

These mountains were home. At least, he wanted them to be. If only what he wanted mattered in this situation.

Grant me peace, Lord. Help me find the right way forward in all this.

Back inside, he couldn't stop himself from checking on her. William's room glowed faintly, the lamp Mrs. Wang had left casting soft shadows across the walls. Their housekeeper must be in the kitchen. Or seeing to Heidi and Two Stones's comfort.

Having guests was always a special treat for Mrs. Wang. So many people to dote on.

He stepped just inside the room where Mrs. Beaumont lay, the rug keeping his boots silent. The woman slept, her chest rising and falling, slow and even, her face peaceful in the flickering light. A bandage wrapped around her head, which hadn't been there before. Was there bleeding that wouldn't stop? Mrs. Wang was an excellent nurse, so she would have known all the steps to take.

The white cloth stood stark against the woman's pale skin, a mark of how close she'd come to disaster. She looked fragile, too delicate for this land. But there was a peace in her stillness, a quiet resilience he couldn't ignore.

He stepped closer, studying her. High cheekbones, a small nose, lips parted slightly in sleep—she was beautiful, no denying it. But beauty didn't mean she'd survive here. What had driven her to answer William's ad? What had she left behind in Savannah to chase a stranger's promise? A spark of curiosity flickered in him, unbidden.

Unwanted.

He shouldn't care, couldn't let her in.

Her lashes fluttered, and he froze. If she woke, she would catch him staring.

She sighed, then shifted under the blankets. He eased out a breath and turned to the door.

Before slipping out, he glanced back for a final look.

Tomorrow, he'd tell her the truth, offer her his name, and let her choose. Ready or not, he'd step into the path ahead.

CHAPTER 7

*P*ain throbbed behind Mandie's eyes, sharp and relentless, yanking her from a sleep she couldn't recall sinking into.

She opened her eyelids, and blurry shapes swam into focus—a strange room of rough-hewn logs. Sunlight slashed through a narrow window, glinting off a quilt that pinned her down, heavy and coarse against her skin.

Not her bed. Her pulse spiked, a frantic drumbeat in her chest. This wasn't her polished four-poster draped in lace in her chamber in the townhouse. Where was she?

She shifted, and a jolt of agony ripped through her skull. Her fingers brushed a bandage, tight and scratchy around her head. Panic surged, bitter on her tongue. The air reeked of woodsmoke and damp earth—nothing like the jasmine-scented parlor in her home.

Birds trilled outside, too loud, too wild, mingling with muffled voices—men, maybe—drifting from somewhere beyond the logs. She squeezed her eyes shut, clawing for a memory.

Her home. Sitting in church with Mama and Papa. The

awful feeling that always came with Clayton's presence. And Nicholas was gone. Lingering sadness pressed at that thought.

She struggled to find a firmer memory. Something recent. But a thick, suffocating fog smothered everything. Why couldn't she remember?

The door creaked, and Mandie flinched, pain flaring like a whipcrack.

A woman stepped in, gray streaking her dark hair, pulled back tight. She carried a wooden tray, and her almond-shaped eyes shone with kindness.

A stranger. Mandie's heart hammered, her hands slick against the quilt.

"Good morning." The woman smiled as she set her tray on the table beside the bed. "I'm Bea Wang, housekeeper here. How are you feeling?"

Mandie's throat scraped dry. "Head hurts." Her voice rasped so much it didn't sound like hers. "Where am I?"

Mrs. Wang dragged a chair closer, and the scrape of wood sent a piercing stab through Mandie's head. The woman settled into the seat, her weathered hands folding in her lap. "You're at the Balfour ranch, in the Montana Territory." Her voice was gentle, but the words hit Mandie like a punch in her middle.

"Montana?" The room spun. "How...Why am I here?"

A flicker of concern crossed Mrs. Wang's face. "What do you remember, child?"

Mandie squeezed her eyes shut, grasping for something, anything. "I...don't know. It's all a blur." Tears pricked hot behind her lids. "My last clear memory is of being with my parents at church. In Savannah." The Montana Territory was so very far away from Georgia. How did she get here?

Mrs. Wang's expression softened, and she reached for a cup on the tray, steam curling from its surface. "Here, this tea will ease the pain."

Mandie struggled to sit up, wincing as the room tilted. Mrs.

Wang steadied her with a gentle hand, helping her sip the fragrant liquid.

The drink soothed her raw throat but did nothing to calm the rising tide of confusion and fear. "I don't understand." Her fingers trembled against the cup. "Why am I here? What happened?"

"You rode from Fort Benton with Two Stones and Heidi, a young couple who trade in these parts. You all stopped for a storm, and afterwards, you slipped on a rock. Cracked your head good. They brought you to us yesterday."

Mandie frowned, chasing shadows in her mind. Two Stones. Heidi. A wagon. A rock. Nothing surfaced—just a maddening fog.

"I don't know them." Her chest squeezed tight. "I don't remember."

The woman rested a hand on hers, warm and rough. "That's fine, dear. You hit hard and healing takes time. Let yourself rest and you'll remember."

She squinted at the woman. "What did you say this ranch is called?"

"The Balfour Ranch. We're about an hour and a half from Walnut Springs, the nearest town. Our closest neighbors are the Jenkins, a nice couple to the south, expecting their first baby in a few weeks. They're still quite a ways from us."

A knock cut the air before Mandie could respond.

A man stepped through the open doorway—tall, broad-shouldered, dark hair spilling over his brow. And a beard concealing every bit of his face from the cheekbones down.

He looked…nearly wild.

His blue eyes pinned her, sharp and searching, and he moved with a stillness that made the room feel smaller.

Her breath snagged, fingers digging into the quilt. Who was he?

"This is Lord Enoch Balfour." Mrs. Wang stood, her skirts rustling. "He's been waiting for you to wake."

"Lord?" The title clanged in Mandie's ears, absurd against these raw logs. Lords belonged in velvet parlors, not...the wilderness territories.

"Just Enoch." He spoke with a voice low and deep. His mouth held a faint curve missing from those piercing eyes. "How are you, Mrs. Beaumont?"

He knew who she was.

She summoned moisture to her dry mouth and glanced between him and Mrs. Wang. "How do you know my name? And how did I get to the Montana Territory?"

He reached for another chair against the wall and pulled it close so he could face her. As he eased into the seat, the wood creaked. "Do you remember anything about the journey? Why you came?"

Did *he* not know? She shut her eyes, reaching. "I...I can't..." She let out a sigh as she opened her eyes. "It's all so murky. I can't find a clear thought."

He nodded, his lips meeting in a line. He seemed to be weighing his next words. Or maybe weighing *her*, like she might break. "You were corresponding with my brother, William. Sound familiar?"

"William?" Nothing—no flicker, no echo. Her chest clenched. "No. Why?"

Enoch's gaze never flickered. And that beard made it hard to see the rest of his expression. "He placed an advertisement for a wife— a mail-order bride—and you answered. You came to marry him."

The words crashed over her, icy and absurd. A mail-order bride? Her, Mandie Beaumont, trading Savannah's parlors for a life so far away in a place she'd never even visited? "That's impossible." Her voice shook. "I wouldn't. Did I know him?"

Enoch's brow furrowed, his gaze searching hers as if trying

to piece together a puzzle. "You never met in person. Just letters."

Her mind reeled, grasping for a shred of logic in this madness. She, who had been perfectly content living on her own after Nicholas died, agreeing to marry a stranger? Impossible.

Mrs. Wang's gentle hand settled on her shoulder. "Perhaps it's best not to push too hard, dear. The memories will come in time."

But she couldn't let it rest, the panic rising like bile in her throat. She fixed Enoch with a desperate stare. "Where is your brother now? I need to speak with him, to understand."

Something flickered in the depths of his eyes, there and gone, shuttered behind an unreadable mask. He glanced at Mrs. Wang, a silent exchange passing between them.

The housekeeper nodded. An encouragement to continue.

A new thread of panic rose in her. What more could there be? Something so bad he considered not telling her. Had she committed to marry a monster? A man with a violent temper? Or worse?

That same awful feeling that came with the memory of Nicholas's brother rose now. Surely she hadn't somehow agreed to marry a fiend like Clayton Beaumont.

Enoch leaned forward, elbows braced on his knees, his large hands clasped. The rough skin and blunt nails spoke of a life of labor, so at odds with the title Mrs. Wang had called him.

"Mrs. Beaumont..." He paused, jaw working beneath his beard. "There's no gentle way to say this." His voice was low, threaded with an undercurrent of something she couldn't grasp. "My brother, William...he passed away more than three months ago. A tragic accident, here on the ranch. I sent word to you, but you must have already left."

The words hung in the air, heavy and suffocating. Mandie stared at him, her mind struggling to make sense of it all. The man she'd supposedly agreed to marry...dead? Before she even arrived?

Grief and confusion and even a bit of relief warred within her, tangling into a knot lodged in her throat. She swallowed hard and met Enoch's weary eyes. She could be relieved not to be forced into a marriage she didn't remember agreeing to—with a stranger, no less.

But he'd lost his brother. Only three months ago. She could only imagine how hard that must be. As an only child, she'd always craved siblings. A brother, especially. Losing him would be devastating.

She swallowed again and managed to speak. "I'm sorry." The words felt hollow, inadequate.

He nodded, his gaze shifting to the window. A heavy silence hung between them, thick with unspoken emotions.

Her mind reeled, trying to grasp the enormity of her situation. She had traveled thousands of miles to marry a man she couldn't remember, only to find him dead. And now she was stranded in this wild, unfamiliar place, with no idea of what the future held.

Mrs. Wang's gentle voice broke through the fog of her thoughts. "Perhaps it's best if we let you rest now. This is a lot to take in all at once."

Enoch nodded, his expression still guarded. He rose from the chair, his tall frame filling the small room. "Of course. We can discuss the details later." He turned to Mandie, his blue eyes softening a fraction. "If you need anything, let Mrs. Wang know. I'll be around the ranch."

With that, he strode from the room, his bootsteps echoing down the hall. Mandie sank deeper into the pillow, exhaustion and confusion weighing heavy on her limbs.

Mrs. Wang fussed with the quilt, tucking it around her. "Don't you worry about a thing, dear. We'll sort this all out. For now, focus on getting your strength back."

Mandie managed a weak smile for the woman's kindness. But as Mrs. Wang bustled out of the room, she let the smile fade. She stared at the rough-hewn ceiling, her thoughts churning like storm-tossed waves.

How had her life come to this? Waking up in a strange bed, in a strange house, in a territory she'd never set foot in before. With no memory of how or why she'd traveled so far from everything familiar.

And now, to learn that the man she'd supposedly agreed to marry was dead...

Her mind drifted to her life back in Savannah, to the genteel society she'd navigated nearly every day. The afternoon teas, the charity bazaars, the endless rounds of calls and social obligations. It had been a life of comfort and privilege, but also one of suffocating expectations.

Especially after Nicholas died. Her throat tightened at the memory of her husband, lost too soon to a fever that swept through the city like a scythe. In the wake of his death, she'd been left adrift, alone in a world that didn't know what to do with a young widow.

And then there had been Clayton, Nicholas's brother, with his sly smiles and grasping hands. He'd made it clear he wanted her and her money—Nicholas's money. The thought of him sent a shudder down her spine.

Perhaps that was why she'd answered William's advertisement. To escape the gilded cage of Savannah society, to flee Clayton's unwanted advances. To start a new life in a place where no one knew her past, where she could be valued for more than her beauty and money.

Now William was gone. What sort of man was his brother, this solemn Lord Enoch with the piercing blue eyes?

It didn't matter. She had no right to impose on this family.

She had to decide what to do next. No matter how much the thought twisted her insides.

Mandie pressed down the nerves churning in her middle as she smoothed her skirt before the mirror. One last time to make sure all was in place before she ventured out of the room.

Bea had said she could join the family for the evening meal if she felt strong enough, and after endless hours staring at these log walls, the prospect of conversation and companionship sounded tempting. Her head barely ached anymore.

Her room was comfortable enough, with a sturdy bed frame, a carved wooden dresser, and a washstand with a thick porcelain basin. But the furnishings held a masculine air, as if they had been chosen for function over form. Was this simply an extra guest chamber? Or had she taken a room from one of the family members?

Inhaling a deep breath, Mandie opened the heavy wooden door and stepped into the dimly lit hallway. The floorboards creaked beneath her feet as she made her way toward the main part of the house.

Rich scents wafted from the kitchen—roasting meat and herbs—and her stomach made an unladylike sound.

As she entered the great room, a tall figure emerged from a side chamber. One of the brothers, but she didn't know his name. Or rather, she'd memorized the names Bea told her, but didn't know which face they matched up to.

Except Enoch, of course. That glimpse of the eldest Balfour had burned him clearly in her memory.

This younger brother looked up and stopped short at the sight of her, his eyes widening.

"Mrs. Beaumont." He quickly collected himself. "It's a pleasure to see you out and about. I trust you're feeling better?"

She offered a smile. "I am, thank you, Mr. Balfour. Bea thought I might be ready to join everyone for dinner." Should she have called him Lord Balfour?

"Please, call me Robert." His eyes crinkled at the corners. "We don't stand much on formality here. And we'll all be glad for your company."

The sound of voices drew her focus to the staircase, where two more Balfour brothers trotted down. These must be James and Thomas. Hadn't Bea said Thomas was the youngest? If so, he must be the darker-haired one. He looked slightly more youthful, though the entire family was a handsome lot. What had William been like? Something fluttered in her middle. Probably as comely as his younger brothers, or maybe more so.

But that didn't matter. William was gone, and his brothers still grieved deeply, no doubt. Where were their parents? Bea had never mentioned them, which made her think the brothers had been on their own for many years.

Thomas led the way, jumping the last two steps to the main floor. He flashed an infectious grin. "Look who's decided to grace us with her presence. Thomas, at your service." He swept into an exaggerated bow, then straightened with a wink, his green eyes laughing. "I'd heard whispers of a beautiful maiden gracing our humble abode, but I dared not believe them until now."

Goodness, what a charmer.

James elbowed him aside. "Pay him no mind, Mrs. Beaumont. He's been reading entirely too much Byron of late. I'm James, and we're delighted you could join us." Taller and broader through the shoulders than Robert or Thomas, he nevertheless shared the same classically handsome features and air of good breeding.

"I suppose I should be flattered to be immortalized in verse." She arched her brows. "Though I shudder to imagine the rhyming words one could concoct for Mandie."

"Mandie." Thomas rolled the syllables around on his tongue as if tasting them. "Why, the possibilities are endless. Candy, dandy, handy...er, perhaps not that last one." He flashed her a cheeky grin.

The taller brother rolled his eyes heavenward. "Please pay no mind to my ridiculous sibling. The rest of us do try to comport ourselves with some modicum of dignity."

She couldn't help a genuine smile. How refreshing to be among people who could laugh and tease without ulterior motives. Perhaps this evening wouldn't be so daunting after all.

A door opened beside the staircase, and Enoch stepped into view, his broad shoulders filling the frame. He must have come from washing up, for his damp hair slicked back from his forehead, and water still glistened on his large, work-stained hands.

He joined the group, his sharp blue gaze fixed on her. "Mrs. Beaumont? Should you be out of bed?"

Up close, she could see the fine lines etched around his eyes and mouth, the weariness that clung to him like a second skin. Her insides gave a tiny flutter, and she had the sudden, mad urge to reach out and smooth the furrow between his dark brows.

But instead, she lifted her chin, meeting his eyes steadily. "Bea said I could join everyone for the evening meal if I felt up to it. And after being confined to bed all day, I find myself quite eager for companionship."

Enoch's head tipped as something like curiosity touched his gaze. But then his expression settled. "I see. Well, if Mrs. Wang thinks it wise..." He trailed off, his gaze flickering over her as if assessing her condition for himself.

James cleared his throat. "We were just welcoming Mrs. Beaumont to the table, Enoch. No need to look so grim about it."

"I'm not grim." Enoch's jaw tightened. "Merely surprised. And concerned for our guest's well-being."

Thomas rolled his eyes. "Come off it, Enoch. The lady says she's feeling better. Let her enjoy a meal without you hovering like a mother hen."

A tense silence fell over the room. Mandie glanced between the brothers, sensing the undercurrents of old resentments and unspoken grief.

Thomas caught her eye and flashed a conspiratorial wink, as if to say, *Don't mind the old bear. We'll have some fun yet.*

Finally, Enoch let out a sigh, his shoulders relaxing a little. "You're right, of course. Forgive me, Mrs. Beaumont. It's not been easy of late." He gestured toward the dining room. "Please, allow me to escort you to the table."

Mandie hesitated only a moment before stepping forward and placing her hand on his offered arm. A very solid, very warm arm. The contact sent an unexpected frisson through her, and she had to force herself to breathe. What was it about this man that unsettled her so?

As they walked the short distance to the dining room, she was acutely aware of his height, the breadth of his shoulders, the way he shortened his stride to match hers.

This was no different than any dinner party back in Savannah.

Yet this wasn't Savannah.

She was being escorted to dinner by a veritable stranger in a sprawling Montana ranch house. Still, somehow this felt comfortable. And pleasant. Maybe even exciting.

He cleared his throat and spoke in a low, almost conversational voice. "Mrs. Wang seems quite taken with you."

She allowed a smile. The housekeeper had brought a tray of fragrant tea and still-warm scones that afternoon. They'd talked for nearly an hour, Bea sharing some of her own history, how she emigrated from China to England as a young girl, then married Mr. Wang and the two came to work for the Balfour family. She'd asked about Mandie's past too, and it had felt good to share. Not all the smaller details, but the main facts. Her parents, her father's governmental work, Nicholas and his death.

Bea's eyes had glistened when Mandie shared that last part, and she'd taken Mandie's hand. *I'm so sorry, dear. I know words don't ease the pain, but I'd love to hear more about him when you're ready.* Both of them were widows, it seemed. One more bond they shared.

"She's been very kind to me. She has a way of seeing what other people miss."

Something shifted in Enoch's expression then, a minute crack in his stoic façade. His arm twitched beneath her hand. "She does." His voice came out a little gruffer than usual. "She's always seen straight through my bluster." One corner of his mouth lifted as he glanced her way.

Not a full smile, but her heart gave a little flip. How would he look if he truly grinned? If he gave himself over to joy or laughter or abandon? A part of her yearned to find out, to dig past the layers of grief and duty and reservation until she unearthed the man beneath.

But those thoughts would only lead downward.

They'd reached the dining room, where the table had been

laid with clean white China and sparkling silver, a bounty that seemed at odds with the rustic simplicity of the house itself.

Enoch paused as he studied the chairs, his brow furrowed as if confronted with a vexing riddle. Then he led her to the chair beside the head and pulled it out for her.

She sank into the proffered seat with a murmur of thanks, watching from the corner of her gaze as Enoch took the seat to her right at the head of the table. He stared at the empty plate before him, as though he'd never seen one like it before.

The younger Balfours filed in behind them, their earlier joviality tempered by something Mandie couldn't quite put a name to. Each eyed Enoch as they found their chairs. Surprise seemed to be the common theme, but she couldn't for the life of her determine why. What had Enoch done so differently tonight than his usual?

James finally broke the charged silence, a slow, speculative smile spreading across his face as he settled into his seat across from her. "About time." He sent her a wink, but didn't explain his cryptic words.

Enoch's jaw tightened, but he said nothing as Bea emerged from the kitchen, bearing a large platter of roast beef, the savory aroma preceding her. She placed it in the center of the table with a flourish, her dark eyes twinkling as she surveyed the gathered family. "Well now, doesn't this make a nice picture? It's been too long since I've seen a lady grace our table."

She settled into the seat nearest the kitchen, and they all bowed their heads. Mandie quickly did the same, and Robert spoke a prayer over the food. Did he always say grace? She was accustomed to the man of the house doing so—first her father, then Nicholas. But Robert was third or fourth in line, as far as she could tell.

When they spoke the "amen," activity commenced before she could even lift her head.

All the brothers reached for the nearest serving spoons and

heaped generous portions onto their plates. Enoch took up the fork for the roast, but placed the first serving on Mandie's dish before scooping a generous chunk onto his own.

As the food made its way around the table, conversation began to flow. James and Thomas regaled her with tales of the spring calves and foals, their words tumbling over each other in their eagerness to share. Robert interjected occasionally to correct an exaggeration or add a salient detail.

And Enoch…Enoch remained largely silent as he listened and ate. But he seemed to relax by degrees, the tight line of his shoulders easing as he listened to his brothers' chatter.

Every so often, his gaze would flicker to her, as if to gauge her reaction to their stories.

She couldn't quite puzzle him out. He was clearly the head of the family and took his responsibilities seriously. But he possessed a heaviness. Was it only grief for his brother lurking beneath the surface? Or did another weight drag down his joy?

Whatever the case, his pain called to something deep within her. She knew what it was to pretend at normalcy while your heart bled in secret.

Bea kept the meal running smoothly, hopping up to fetch a second helping of potatoes or refill a water glass. The food was delicious—simple but hearty fare that warmed Mandie to her toes.

As the meal drew to a close, Mandie dabbed at the corners of her mouth with her napkin, feeling more sated and content than she had all day. The Balfour brothers' easy camaraderie and Bea's warm hospitality had worked their magic, soothing the raw edges of her grief and uncertainty.

She still had no idea how or why she'd come here, but for the first time since waking up after the accident, deep in the fog of confusion, a flicker stirred inside her of something that felt a lot like hope.

CHAPTER 9

*E*noch's pulse thrummed like he faced a rattler. The burning afternoon sun pierced his shirt-sleeves as he strode toward the ranch house. He tugged his hat lower, shielding his eyes from the glare. He never came in this early from the pastures, but he had something important to accomplish.

He'd wrestled with this decision all night, then spent all morning planning what he'd say to Mrs. Beaumont. The words looped through his mind until they'd worn a groove deep as a wagon rut.

A sharp squawk jolted him from his thoughts. His gaze snapped to the coop, tucked in between the barn and cellar. Had a snake or fox crept in?

He turned his steps and pushed into a jog. Something had definitely entered the pen. The hens flapped and screeched with an outrage that could scare off any varmint.

As he approached, a dark figure shifted in the shadows of a back corner. A large creature. A bear?

"Enoch!"

The "bear" called his name in a relieved tone that sounded

far too lady-like for a chicken coop, even laced with a tinge of fear.

What in the wide blue sky was *she* doing in there? Shouldn't she still be tucked in bed?

When he reached the doorway and peered inside, he got his first full view of the situation.

There, cornered against the chicken wire, stood Mrs. Beaumont. Her chignon had come loose, dark tendrils curling around her flushed face.

She wielded a basket in one hand, the other clutching her skirts high enough to reveal yards of lace and boots more suited for a dance floor than a henhouse.

Their large red rooster blocked her path—its hackles raised in challenge.

For a moment, Enoch could only stare, caught between amusement and admiration. Mandie's dark hair, usually meticulously coiffed, now fell in damp tendrils around her flushed face. Her eyes flashed with a mix of fear and anger as she swatted at the rooster with her basket.

Enoch's mouth twitched. He shouldn't find amusement in her predicament, but there was something about the way she faced off against that cocksure rooster, her chin lifted, her eyes narrowed in determination.

He shouldn't just stand here and watch though. "Need help?"

Her glare lifted to him. "If you please. He keeps going for my throat."

His grin was getting harder to hold back, so he ducked his chin as he stepped into the pen's slippery muck. "Here now, Rusty." He kept his voice steady and his shoulders squared. "That's no way to treat a lady."

The rooster swung its beady gaze toward him, puffing its chest in a display of bravado.

Enoch chuckled and scooped up the bird like he'd done a hundred times before.

Rusty squawked indignantly, but settled as Enoch stroked its feathers.

"There." He softened his voice for the rooster as he met Mrs. Beaumont's startled gaze over Rusty's bright red comb. "No harm done."

She straightened, smoothing her skirts, and sent them both another glare. The basket trembled in her hands though. Had she really been frightened?

He moved to the side and motioned for her to pass through the door. Once she stepped outside, he freed the rooster to run with the hens, then followed Mrs. Beaumont out and secured the latch behind him.

At last, he turned to walk with her toward the house. "Sorry. Rusty's guarding his hens."

She sent him a sideways look, but she seemed to have regained her composure. "I see that." Her voice held a touch of frost, but the corners of her lips twitched. "Bea asked me to gather a few eggs so we could make a custard. I didn't expect to be ambushed."

He let his gaze skim over her. Even with dirt smudged on her cheek and her dress wrinkled from the tussle, she was beautiful—too beautiful for him to linger on. Her brown eyes caught the sunlight, warm and deep, and a stray curl framed her face like a painter's stroke.

But he pushed that thought aside. "How're you feeling? I'm surprised to see you up and about so soon."

She lifted her chin. "Much better, thank you. The fresh air and activity are doing me good." Her expression clouded. "I only wish I would get my memories back."

His gut clenched. He'd been hoping she'd started to recall details. It would make this conversation a sight easier. "Well, no need to rush it. I'm sure it'll all come back to you in time."

She nodded, but the furrow remained between her brows.

They'd reached the porch steps. Enoch cleared his throat.

"Actually, I was hoping I might have a word with you, if you're up to it."

She turned to face him, her expression guarded. "Of course. What is it you wish to discuss?"

He gestured toward the porch chairs. "Can we sit?"

A flicker of uncertainty crossed her features, but she nodded. "Let me take these eggs to Bea first." She gestured to the basket on her arm. "And perhaps tidy up a bit." A wry smile touched her lips as she glanced down at her disheveled appearance.

"Certainly." He dipped his chin. "I'll wait for you here."

As she disappeared into the house, he leaned against the porch railing, his nerves stretched tight. He'd faced down possessive mother cows and even a grizzly once, but this conversation had his pulse pounding like a spooked colt.

He turned and gazed out over the ranch, the land that had shaped him into the man he was—that tethered him to this place even as duty pulled him toward a distant shore. This sunbaked earth and snow-capped peaks were as much a part of him as the blood in his veins.

The creak of the door sounded, and he straightened as Mrs. Beaumont stepped out. She'd tidied her hair and smoothed her skirts, but a smudge of dirt still lingered on her cheek. It made her seem more real somehow, less like a fine lady and more like a woman who could stand at his side, facing the challenges of this rugged land.

As she approached, he couldn't bring himself to sit. Instead, he gripped the rough-hewn railing, the wood solid beneath his fingers.

She moved to stand beside him at the railing, leaving a respectable distance between them. Her eyes followed his gaze to the mountains. "It's beautiful here," she said softly. "Peaceful."

He nodded, not trusting his voice yet. The words he'd practiced had fled like startled quail. He cleared his throat. "Mrs.

Beaumont, I wanted to tell you a bit about our family, if that's all right."

Her brow furrowed, but she nodded. "Of course."

He took a steadying breath. "My father is the Duke of Clarence, in England. Our family...we've faced threats as far back as I can remember. It started when Will and I were just lads." He hesitated, the old wounds stirring. "Our father's cousin, Reginald, wanted the title for himself. He saw us as obstacles—Will, me, James, and then Robert. Thomas wasn't born yet."

Mandie's brow furrowed, her eyes flickering with curiosity and concern as she leaned against the porch rail.

"He tried to tear our family down at first by attacking our mother." Bitterness crept into his tone, so he worked to soften it. "She was Scottish, with Catholic loyalties—a detail the Church of England strongly opposed. Reginald claimed it made her unfit to be a duchess, that it tainted our legitimacy as heirs. He spread rumors, even took it to the courts, hoping to have us disinherited. But our father's influence was stronger, and Reginald's lies fell apart."

Mandie's hand tightened on the rail, her knuckles whitening. "What did he do then?"

Enoch's jaw clenched, the memory cutting deeper. "He turned desperate. He had Will kidnapped—snatched him right from our estate. Held him for a day before our father's men tracked him down and brought him back."

His voice roughened, the fear of that day seeping back like a fist gripping his chest. "Will was so young... I can still hear our mother's cries when we realized he was gone. That was the breaking point. Our father sent her and us here to Montana with a handful of trusted staff to protect us from Reginald." He paused, the ache of the upheaval tightening his chest. "It was supposed to be temporary."

Mandie's eyes widened at the initial revelation, but they

softened with each layer he peeled back. Now, her voice turned gentle. "That must have been so hard."

He gave a small nod, memories of those early days flitting through his mind—the confusion, the fear, the glimpses of his mother's tears when she thought no one was watching. "I guess it was. We were uprooted, sent across an ocean to a place we didn't understand. But it kept us alive."

Mandie touched his arm. "You've been through so much."

For a moment, he couldn't find words. He met her gaze, her eyes giving more than sympathy. They held a quiet strength that steadied him.

He pulled his gaze away. He had to focus on the next most important part of the conversation. "Eventually, this land, this life...it became a part of us." He met her gaze, willing her to understand. "Will, though—he always knew he'd go back some-day, to take up the mantle of the dukedom. He was preparing for it, before..." His throat closed around the words.

Her hand squeezed his arm. "Before he died."

He swallowed and shifted his thoughts past that point. "The plan was for him to marry, then travel to England to be intro-duced at Parliament and learn the role of a duke from our father." The words felt heavy on his tongue, weighted with the responsibility that now fell to him.

A frown pulled on her face, like she was trying to under-stand. "Did I know he was...a duke? Or would become one?" She gave her head a little shake. "I mean, did I know he wanted a wife who would go with him to England and be..."

The knot in his middle pulled a little tighter as he finished her question. "...his duchess? I honestly don't know if Will told you or not. I found the letter you sent him, but I'm not sure what he wrote to you." He raised his brows. "Perhaps you have them? In your luggage?"

Her mouth pinched. "I only found one note. He suggested that I come and visit first, so the two of us could become acquainted. Then we could both decide if we wanted to proceed with…marriage." Did her voice quiver on that last word?

He turned back to stare at the trees ahead. "That sounds like Will. He was usually hesitant to mention our title—we've all kept quiet about it. He might have wanted to tell you in person, then give you ample time to decide."

She nodded slowly, her gaze distant as if trying to grasp memories just out of reach. "I wish I could remember more about our correspondence, about what led me to make this journey." Frustration edged her voice.

If only he had the right words to ease her mind, but he was fumbling in the dark himself.

She met his gaze again. "So what happens now?"

He turned to face her fully. "With Will gone, that responsibility falls to me, as the next eldest son. I'll need to marry and travel to England, to learn the estates and what it means to be the Duke of Clarence." The words felt like splintering wood in his throat, scraping against the life he'd built here, the man he'd become.

Her eyes widened, but she held his gaze. "I see." Her voice was soft, laced with a note of something he couldn't quite decipher. Sympathy? Uncertainty?

He steeled himself, his heart pounding against his ribs. "Mrs. Beaumont, I find myself in need of a wife. And you…you would make a fine duchess."

He forced himself to hold her gaze, to not look away from the surprise and uncertainty in her eyes. "Would you consider marrying me, knowing all this? Knowing the life it would entail?"

Mandie stared at him, her expression unreadable save for the widening of her eyes. Seconds ticked by, each one an eternity as he waited for her response. His lungs pressed so hard, only a little breath seeped in and out.

At last, she looked away, her gaze drifting to the mountains that had become his home, his sanctuary. "I...don't know what to say." Her voice barely rose above a whisper, carried away on the summer breeze.

His heart sank, but he forced himself to nod. "I understand. It's a lot to take in." He tried to keep his tone steady, not let the disappointment bleed through.

She turned back to him, her dark eyes searching his face. "It's not only that. I still don't know why I came here, why I agreed to be a mail-order bride in the first place. I feel like I'm missing a piece of myself." Her hand rose to her temple as if she could physically grasp the memories that eluded her.

His body tightened. If only he could reach out and offer comfort, but he held himself back. She likely wouldn't appreciate contact between them. "I know. And I don't want to pressure you. We're both in a difficult position."

She nodded, her gaze dropping to her clasped hands. "I appreciate your candor, Mr. Balfour. And your offer. I just...I need some time. To think, to try to remember." She looked up at him, her eyes pleading for understanding.

He nodded, even as disappointment gnawed at his middle. "Of course. Take all the time you need."

She gave him a small, grateful smile. Then she stepped back from the rail. "I should go help Bea with the custard." She turned and moved with her measured stride toward the front door.

"Mrs. Beaumont." Her name escaped his lips before he could stop it.

She paused, glancing back at him.

He swallowed, his throat dry. "I know this is a lot to consider. But please know that I would strive to be a good husband to you. To provide for you and protect you, always." The words sounded stilted to his own ears, but he needed her to understand.

Her expression softened. "I don't doubt that, Mr. Balfour.

You've shown me nothing but kindness since I arrived." She hesitated, as if weighing her next words. "I need to be certain it's the right path though. For both of us."

With that, she slipped into the house, leaving him alone on the porch with the turmoil of his thoughts.

He turned back to the mountains, their peaks stretching up into the clouds. He'd always found solace in their steadfast presence, but now they only reminded him of the uncertainties looming before him.

England. The dukedom. A wife. They were all part of a life he'd never wanted, a role he'd never asked for.

Yet here he stood, disappointed that his first step on this new path hadn't been a resounding victory.

CHAPTER 10

andie sat at the dining table the next morning, cradling a porcelain teacup as she breathed in the faint scent of chamomile.

The brothers dug into breakfast, forks clinking against plates of eggs and bacon, their voices a lively tangle of laughter and teasing.

Bea hummed softly in the kitchen amidst the rhythmic clatter of a wooden spoon against a pot.

Mandie shifted in her chair, the ache behind her eyes still pulsing a little—a stubborn echo of her injury. She sipped her tea, the warmth soothing her throat, and watched the brothers.

Back in Savannah, breakfast had been a hushed affair, full of starched linens, polished silver, and the murmurs of polite conversation…lacking that last bit after Nicholas passed.

Here, it was all noise and motion—James wiping grease from his chin, Thomas gesturing with a biscuit, Robert nodding along like a patient oak. She felt like a sparrow among hawks, out of place yet oddly drawn to their rugged warmth.

Enoch sat to her right, his broad shoulders a steady anchor.

He caught her eye and tipped his head, voice low. "Sleep all right?"

"Well enough." She kept her tone soft with the smooth, careful diction her mother had drilled into her. Yet further small talk fled her mind.

His proposal from yesterday hung like a shadow—she'd have to give him an answer soon. But marrying a man she didn't know? She couldn't fathom why she would have planned to do so in the first place. And until she knew every reason, she couldn't make such a rash decision.

She needed to send a telegram to her parents, figure out why she'd come to this wild place. They might not even know where she was, might be sick with worry for her safety.

Mandie cleared her throat. "I was wondering if one of you might be willing to take me to town. I need to send a note to my family. They may be worried about me."

Enoch's brow furrowed. "It's a long ride, and you're still recovering. But one of us can take the message to the telegraph office for you."

Mandie hesitated. That should suffice, at least for a start. "Thank you. I suppose that will do for now."

Bea slipped in, setting a basket of fresh biscuits on the table. "Eat something, Mandie. You're still too pale."

Mandie offered a small smile, reaching for a biscuit she didn't want. "Thank you, Bea. It smells heavenly." She broke off a small piece, nibbling to please the housekeeper, though her stomach churned—probably from the lingering dizziness.

A sharp thud of hooves sounded outside, and all four men froze mid-bite. The sound pounded closer until it rattled the windowpanes.

Enoch rose first, his chair scraping as he stepped to the window. "Mr. Jenkins." Tension laced his voice.

Mandie's pulse quickened. Wasn't that the surname of the woman Bea had said she would go help with her birthing when the time came? A visit from her husband this early in the morning couldn't be good.

Enoch strode into the great room, and Mandie rose and followed with the others.

He pulled open the front door just as Mr. Jenkins reached the porch.

The man's face was pale, his eyes wide with urgency. "It's Mary. The baby's coming early. Her pains have started."

Bea stepped forward, wiping her hands on her apron. "I'll get my things. James, will you saddle my horse, please?" Without waiting for an answer, she turned and hurried toward her chamber.

As his brother trotted through the door toward the barn, Enoch turned to Mr. Jenkins. "You're in good hands with Mrs. Wang. I'm sure Mary and the baby will be fine."

Mr. Jenkins attempted a smile, but it came out as more of a grimace. "It's our first. I just hope…" He didn't finish, but the twisting in his expression showed the progression of worries likely parading through his thoughts.

Mandie stepped forward. "We'll be praying for them both. For you all."

Mr. Jenkins glanced at her, seeming to notice her presence for the first time. He gave a short nod, some of the tension easing from his shoulders. "Thank you, Miss…?"

"Beaumont. Mrs. Mandie Beaumont." She curtsied out of habit. "I'm a guest of the Balfours."

A flicker of curiosity flashed in his eyes, but Bea returned then, pulling his attention. Enoch took the carpetbag from her hands, and Bea turned to Mandie. "I shouldn't leave you here alone, not while you're still recovering."

"I'll be fine." Mandie gave her a reassuring smile. "I'm feeling much stronger. Please, go help Mrs. Jenkins. She needs you more than I do right now."

Bea searched her face, then nodded. "Very well. But promise to rest and not overexert yourself."

"I promise." Mandie gave a solid nod. "We'll be praying for a safe delivery."

"I'll make sure she rests." Enoch spoke with a firm tone. "You focus on Mary and the babe. We'll manage here."

Bea's eyes softened as she looked between them. "I know you will."

She turned to Mr. Jenkins. "Let's be off then."

As she strode through the open front door, Mr. Jenkins locked gazes with Enoch. "I'll bring her back safe and sound, soon as the baby's here and Mary's on the mend."

Enoch nodded. "We'll pray all goes well."

They followed Mr. Jenkins outside, where James was already helping Bea up into the saddle of a sturdy brown mare. Enoch tied on the carpetbag, then the pair rode off.

As the hoofbeats faded, a charged silence settled over their group.

Enoch's jaw worked beneath his beard, his gaze distant as if his thoughts had followed Bea and Mr. Jenkins down the trail. After a long moment, he seemed to shake himself, his focus snapping back to the present. "I suppose we'd best get to work."

Robert nodded and turned to the house. "I'll clean up from breakfast."

Thomas hesitated, his gaze flickering to Mandie. "Will you be all right on your own, Mrs. Beaumont? I could stay behind, keep you company."

Mandie offered a faint smile. "I'll be fine, thank you. I'm sure I can find ways to occupy myself."

Enoch eyed his remaining younger brothers. "You two go check on the broodmare, then let's get started on the saddle horses."

As they ambled toward the barn, Enoch turned to her and spoke in a gentler tone. "You should rest now. I can have one of the men take your message to town later. It's been an eventful morning."

Mandie lifted her chin. "I'm not an invalid, Mr. Balfour. A bit of excitement won't send me to my sickbed."

A ghost of a smile touched his lips. "No, I don't suppose it would." He stepped closer, his gaze searching her face. "But you *are* still recovering. Please, take it easy today. For Mrs. Wang's peace of mind, if not for mine."

His nearness sent a flutter through her middle, but she tamped it down. "Very well. But I need to write the telegram first."

He studied her a moment, as if weighing her resolve. Then he nodded. "There's paper and ink in the study."

"Thank you." She meant it, truly. For his understanding, his care. It relieved her even as uncertainty still churned in her middle.

As she turned to head into the house, his deep voice stopped her. "Mrs. Beaumont..."

She glanced back and found him watching her with an intensity that made her breath catch.

"I know I asked a lot of you yesterday. And I understand your hesitation. But please know, you'll be safe here, cared for, no matter what you decide."

Emotion welled in her throat, threatening her composure. She managed a nod. "I do know that. And I'm grateful, truly."

His jaw tightened, but he said nothing more as she slipped away, her skirts whispering against the plank floor.

In the study, she sank into the large wooden chair behind the desk. Her fingers trembled as she reached for the pen and paper. The weight of her situation pressed on her chest, making each breath an effort.

She dipped the nib in the ink well and poised it over the blank page. What could she possibly say to her parents to explain her predicament? That she had traveled across the country to marry a stranger, but now found herself a guest of his equally unknown brother, a man who had just proposed to her himself? It sounded like the plot of a penny dreadful novel.

Mandie closed her eyes and inhaled deeply, trying to still the tumult of her thoughts. Somehow she had to condense it all to a short telegram message.

When she opened them again, she began to write in careful script:

DEAREST MOTHER AND FATHER STOP WRITING FROM MONTANA TERRITORY STOP HAVE SUFFERED INJURY AND MEMORY LOSS STOP BEING CARED FOR BY BALFOUR FAMILY STOP PLEASE ADVISE REASON FOR MY JOURNEY STOP YOUR LOVING DAUGHTER MANDIE FULL STOP

As she read over the message, her vision blurred. This short note barely scratched the surface of all she needed to say, all she needed to ask.

But it would have to do for now.

She replaced the pen and leaned back in the chair, her gaze drifting to the window. Outside, the ranch hummed with activity—the distant lowing of cattle, the rhythmic thud of an axe chopping wood, the call of one of the men as the brothers went about their work.

It all felt so foreign, so far removed from the life she knew.

Yet a part of her whispered that perhaps this was exactly where she was meant to be. That maybe, just maybe, there was a reason for her journey, for her arrival at this particular place and time.

Her chest tightened at the thought of Enoch's proposal, his earnest blue eyes searching hers as he spoke of duty and honor and a future she couldn't quite picture. He was a good man, that much was clear. A man who would care for her and protect her.

He might be a touch grumpy, but that made his smiles even more fun to tease out.

What if she stayed here? What if she said yes?

As far-fetched as the idea seemed, she could almost imagine what happiness would look like in this place.

CHAPTER 11

Rain pounded against Enoch's body as he slowed his horse at the barn doors, then jumped to the ground to open one wide enough for his and Thomas's horses to enter.

The storm had descended without warning, a torrent of rain and wind whipping across the pasture where the two of them mended a fence. They'd ridden hard for the barn, the horses' hooves churning the rapidly muddying ground.

A clap of thunder sounded as he closed the barn door behind the horses, and his gelding jerked its head up with the sound.

"Never seen a storm roll in that fast." Thomas led his horse to its stall.

Enoch did the same, moving down to the end of the row. "Hope the others are back." Robert had taken Mandie's telegram to town, and James rode out to the north pasture, the fenced land farthest from the house.

It took little more than a minute to strip the tack and settle the horses. Especially since Robert and Thomas had cleaned the stalls and thrown fresh hay as part of their chores that morning.

"Ready to make a run for it?" He met Thomas at the barn door.

At his brother's nod, Enoch pushed it open, and they both jogged up to the house.

Lightning split the sky as they reached the porch, and thunder crashed the next second. He took the steps in two strides, then slowed on the porch to catch his breath and take off his wet gear.

He shook off his hat, then bent to pull off his boots. Were she here, Mrs. Wang would send him back outside if he stepped foot on the rug with so much dark mud coating his shoes.

Even though he'd worn a hat, the driving wind had soaked his beard, which dripped water down into his shirt collar. His clothes were plastered to his skin. Probably not a suitable condition for a lady to see, but this was the nature of ranch life.

Hopefully he wouldn't meet Mrs. Beaumont on the way to his room. Especially since he only wore stockings.

As he and Thomas were still prying off their muddy boots on the porch, the door swung open, and the woman herself stood in the frame.

"You're both soaked through. Come in and get warm."

She looked far too pretty...and far too fancy in her lace-trimmed dress compared to their bedraggled, mud-soaked clothes. He kicked off his last shoe, then followed Thomas inside. "We'd best get out of these wet clothes first. The others back?"

"Robert's in the study and James is drying off too."

He studied her expression. "Did your telegram get an answer?" If she'd heard from her parents, communicated her injury, would they be coming?

She shook her head and showed only a little disappointment. "He waited an hour, but my parents must have been out."

He nodded. "Every so often, a telegram goes awry out here." He focused on pushing off his last boot.

Mandie stepped aside for them to enter the house. "After

you're both changed, come to the kitchen. I have warm tea and biscuits ready."

When he reached his room, he stripped off his soaked shirt, the stubborn fabric clinging to his skin. In its wake, gooseflesh prickled his arms.

He reached for a dry shirt from his drawer and pushed his hands into the sleeves.

A shout sounded from the front of the house, but the pounding rain drowned out the word.

He tensed, listening so he could make out anything else.

"The barn's on fire!"

His blood turned to ice, and he jerked the shirt over his head as he pushed for the door. He sprinted down the hall, toward the front door.

Thomas was running down the stairs. Good. A glance through the front window showed red mixed with the brown of the barn, but with the sheeting rain, he couldn't make out more.

God, no! If lightning struck the barn directly, all that dry hay might go up in flames before the rain could douse the fire.

He jerked open the door, then forced himself to stop and push his feet into his boots before charging down the stairs and to the barn. They had to get the stock out, then stop the fire from spreading.

Someone must already be working to free the horses, for the barn doors stood wide open.

He raced inside, barely registering the searing heat that hit him like a physical blow. Flames licked across the ceiling, consuming the dry timber with terrifying speed. It had started in the loft as he'd suspected, and now a large hole in the roof was allowing rain over that section.

Maybe it would douse enough fire to stop the blaze's advance.

Smoke was already pushing lower in the air, stinging his eyes and lungs. James led Robert's mare out of the closest stall.

Enoch aimed for the next stall down where they'd been keeping one of the three-year-olds in training that had injured itself. The gash had started to fester, so he wanted the animal close so they could apply salve twice a day.

That stall door already stood open though, and he peered into the darkness to see if the animal was still inside. A person stood with the gelding, reaching high to wrap a rope around the frightened animal's neck.

Mandie.

What was she doing? Between the flames and the panicked horses, she would get hurt—maybe killed.

He charged in to help and reached for the rope she'd managed to secure. "I'll take him. Get back to the house."

"Go help the rest of the horses. I've got him." She pushed Enoch aside with her body as she tugged the horse forward.

The woman had pluck. And maybe she wasn't a greenhorn with horses, for the colt took a tentative step forward.

If she could handle this one, he could go save the other three animals. He stepped around the pair to the stall door. "Once you get him out, stay there with him."

She might be hard-headed, but he didn't have time to mollycoddle her.

Robert was working to get Enoch's gelding out, so he moved down to the broodmare in the last stall. Willow was due to foal any day. Hopefully this ordeal wouldn't put her into early labor. This was to be her first foal since they purchased her, and he had high hopes for the offspring.

He grabbed a rope and jerked the stall's latch open. As he pulled the door wide, he sent a glance upward to see the fire's progress. On the back wall—not far from where he stood—the flames were eating down the wall. The ceiling hadn't fully burned through there, so the inner side of the wood was still dry.

God, stop the fire. Please.

The last thing they needed was to have to rebuild the barn from the ground up. A new roof would be hard enough. And what if the flames leaped to the chicken coop?

He forced his focus back to the mare crowding the rear corner as he stepped into the stall. "Easy, girl. Let's get you out of here."

He approached with the rope, but Willow's eyes rolled white with terror. The smoke was thicker here, and the roar of the flames louder. Sweat ran down his back beneath his damp shirt.

When he reached the mare, he slipped the rope over her neck, then moved the cord higher to a position where he would have more leverage. "All right, girl. Come out where you'll be safe."

He tugged the line, but she balked, throwing her head up. "Easy, girl."

A flash of light outside the stall made her jerk back, and Enoch spun to see the source. A timber fell from the roof, landing on the packed dirt. Flames still licked the fallen wood. Willow probably wouldn't step foot from her stall with the fire right in front of the opening.

He left the horse and strode from the box to kick the wood out of the way. When his boot struck the timber, it skidded across the barn floor, embers scattering in its wake. He should stop and put the flames out, but they had to get the horses free before he fought the fire.

As he turned back to the stall, a cracking sound split the air.

He looked up as another burning timber dropped from the ceiling. He couldn't make his feet move fast enough, but his body twisted sideways as he scrambled out of the way of the falling wood.

Pain exploded across the back of his head and his left shoulder and spine as the timber slammed into him, forcing him to his knees. Heat seared his ear, and he rolled, frantic to get away from the flames. Were they going out? He could only feel oppressive heat. Had his shirt caught fire? His hair? His beard? The haze of smoke clouded around him, clogging his mind and chest.

Hands pulled at him, lifting him. He fought to get his feet underneath him. His left arm ached like the skin had been scraped off with a knife, but he used his other hand to swipe over his head and make sure no flames still lingered.

His hair crinkled, but that might have been straw he'd picked up from the barn floor.

He was on his feet now with his brother gripping one arm.

He shook Robert away, walking on his own. "Are all the horses out?" Maybe he should tell his brother to leave them. They couldn't risk Robert getting caught by falling wood either.

"Mrs. Beaumont has the last one."

If he was a swearing man, those words would have brought on a curse. "Get her out of here!" The smoke made his voice rasp.

He couldn't let her get hurt. He turned back to find the woman himself, but Robert grabbed his good shoulder. "She's coming. There."

Enoch blinked to clear the smoke from his eyes. When he opened them, Mandie was leading the broodmare he'd been trying to free. Willow walked beside her, though the mare's nostrils and eyes flared wide with each step.

Enoch let the pair pass, then trudged toward the barn door with Robert. Men's voices shouted outside.

He forced himself to stand straighter. To walk faster. Now that the animals were safe, they had to do everything possible to put out the flames.

CHAPTER 12

andie's eyes stung as she stumbled into the house. The bedraggled Balfour brothers filed in behind her, and a glance at them all showed they were as dirty as she and must be just as exhausted. They'd finally put out the last of the fire, and the steady patter of rain would hopefully douse the remaining coals and smoke. The lightning had stopped, and they'd caught all the horses from the barn and secured them in the pasture nearest the house.

In the morning, there would be more to do, but for now, they could clean up and rest.

She sent a look toward Enoch. He must be worried about the loss of the barn. His head and shoulders sagged with more exhaustion than the others. Probably a great deal of pain too.

She could still see him in her mind, knocked to the barn floor with flames leaping from his hair and shirt.

He must have terrible burns. If they weren't cleaned and treated, they would fester quickly.

Bea wasn't here, so Mandie should be the one to tend him. Or at least make sure the job was done correctly.

She turned to him, keeping her voice low. "Enoch, your burns need bandaging. Tonight, before infection sets in."

Enoch lifted his head slowly, as if the very act of meeting her gaze required monumental effort. The weariness in his eyes, the tightness around his mouth, spoke volumes of the agony he was enduring.

He shook his head. "I'll manage." His voice scratched so much the words were hard to make out.

She stepped closer to him. "You can't properly clean and bandage the burns yourself. Not when they're on your neck and back." She kept her tone brisk, matter-of-fact. "Go change, then come to the kitchen. I'll take care of it."

Surprise flickered across his face, followed by a flash of something harder to define. "You don't need to bother yourself. It won't be pretty."

She shook her head. "I'm sure it won't. But I've plenty of experience with such. Back home, I often tended injuries for our staff. Burns from the kitchen fires, cuts from a slipped knife or broken glass. I can clean and bandage as well as a doctor." In truth, she always liked being helpful in that way. Making hurting people feel better.

Enoch regarded her for a long moment. His shoulders had stiffened, and for a second, he looked like he would argue. At last, he gave a slow dip of his chin. "Fine." Then he turned and disappeared down the hallway to his chamber.

A small victory, but a vital one. Those burns wouldn't wait on stubborn pride.

Mandie hurried to her room to change out of her sodden, sooty dress and clean the worst of the grime from her face and hands. By the time she reached the kitchen, Enoch was already seated at the table, his head cradled in his uninjured hand.

At her entrance, he looked up, and she nearly stumbled to a halt.

He was shirtless, the broad expanse of his shoulders and

chest bare except for a blanket draped over his uninjured side. The lamplight played over the ridges and planes of his muscled shoulder and chest, highlighting both the power of his form and the vulnerability of his current state.

He met her gaze with weary blue eyes. "Figured you couldn't tend the shoulder if I put a clean shirt on." His voice still rasped with pain and exhaustion. Likely smoke too.

She swallowed and forced herself to nod, then move past the table to the stove behind him. Of course she'd seen a man's bare chest before—she'd been married to Nicholas for three years. But he'd been slender and finely built, his frame honed by a life of privilege and ease.

Enoch Balfour was another creature entirely, all rugged strength and coiled intensity.

She forced her focus onto her work. She was here to provide medical care, not gawk like a schoolgirl. The kettle of water she'd been warming for tea still sat on the stove, so she poured some into a clean basin, tempering it with cool water until the liquid was warm but not scalding.

She had seen a basket on the shelf containing clean cloths, bandages, and a jar of healing salve. Mandie pulled it down and grabbed a towel, then carried it all to the table beside Enoch.

Once more, she was faced with his bare skin and hulking frame, yet standing behind him, she could see the ring of soot around his neck and the burn marks on his shoulder. They didn't look to be open wounds, so hopefully they would heal without trouble.

Dipping the cloth in the warm water, she started on the unburned skin of his neck and shoulder. He tensed at the first touch but didn't flinch away.

"I'm sorry if I hurt you," she murmured.

"S'all right," he ground out. "Do what needs doing."

Working in gentle strokes, she removed the layers of soot and grime, then assessed the damage. The burn on his shoulder wasn't too deep, but the one on his scalp looked far more serious, the skin raw and blistered. "I'm going to need to cut your hair. To treat the burn."

"Fine." The word was little more than a pained exhale.

Mandie took a deep breath to steady her hands, then replaced the cloth in the water and retrieved the scissors from the basket. She fingered a section of longer locks that hung over his neck. His hair was thick and wavy, the rich brown color glinting with hints of auburn in the lamplight. She let herself enjoy the sensation of those silken strands sliding between her fingers.

She had to work though.

With careful strokes, she trimmed away the singed and matted hair around the burn, letting the dark strands fall to the floor. She'd never cut a man's hair before. Never expected the act to feel so intimate.

The hair had to be trimmed everywhere so it would lie evenly, so she moved to his right side to work. Her fingers wove through his thick locks, brushing against his scalp.

Enoch sat completely still beneath her ministrations. Was that because of pain? Or did he feel the connection in this simple act?

This close, with the heat of him radiating against her skin, she was far too aware of Enoch as a man. Not just a patient, not just someone who had extended kindness to her and was in need of aid, but a flesh-and-blood male with all that strong, masculine power.

Bit by bit, the dark waves fell away, leaving his hair cropped close to his head. The shorter layers outlined his strong features, making something flip in her middle. He looked somehow younger, more vulnerable. Only his beard still covered him like armor.

At last, she set the shears aside and reached for the salve. As she smoothed the ointment over the burned patch of scalp, the muscles in his shoulders bunched and twitched.

Her chest tightened and she kept her strokes as light as possible. If only there was a way to take his pain away completely.

She finished his scalp, then moved down to dab the balm over the lesser burns on his shoulder. "Is there anywhere else that hurts?" She kept her voice soft, but it sounded loud in the stillness of the room.

He shook his head. "Just there."

She smoothed the last of the salve over his shoulder, letting her fingers linger a moment longer than necessary. The urge to soothe, to comfort—and yes, to touch this man—was far too strong within her.

Finally, she made herself step back and wipe her hands on the rag. Then she reached for a bandage from the basket and unrolled a length of clean cloth. "I'm going to wrap your head, to keep the salve in place and keep the wound clean while it heals."

He didn't answer. He might not appreciate the attention having his head bandaged would bring, but getting dirt in the open burn would cause trouble.

She worked quickly, then tied off the cloth and shifted around to his side to check her work from that angle. It would do.

She glanced at his face. His eyes were closed, face tight against the pain.

Her chest clenched at the sight. She had to resist the urge to smooth her fingers over the furrow between his brows, to see if she could ease some of his suffering with her touch.

Instead, she spoke in a soft voice. "All done."

His eyes opened, those deep blue depths fixing on her. The weariness in his gaze had deepened, but there was something else there too—a flicker of gratitude…and more. "Thank you." His voice came low, rough with exhaustion and pain.

She nodded. She was standing too close to him. So close she could feel his heat. Or maybe that was her own cheeks flaming. She took a step away. "Of course. It's the least I can do."

She busied herself tidying away the supplies and basin of water while she worked to compose herself. When she turned back, he was still watching her, an unreadable expression on his face.

"We'll need to put more salve on your head two or three times a day. You should rest now." She managed a smile. "The salve will help with the pain and prevent infection, but sleep is the real healer."

He held her gaze a moment longer, then dipped his chin. Bracing his good arm on the table, he pushed to his feet, moving stiffly. She fought the instinct to reach out and steady him.

"Goodnight then. And…thank you, again." With that, he made his way out of the kitchen.

All she could do was stand there and watch him walk through the front door.

* * *

ENOCH STOOD ALONE in the barn after everyone else had retired to their rooms.

The acrid smell of smoke lingered despite the rain. Moonlight streamed through the damaged roof, illuminating the wreckage.

His shoulder and head ached, but nothing compared to the turmoil in his heart.

Mandie's face—pale, determined, framed by the flames—still flashed through his mind. She'd risked herself to save the mare, and he'd nearly lost her.

He sank onto a bucket, his voice a hoarse whisper in the

silence. "Lord, I can't lose her too." He clenched his fists against the memories that surged forward of Charlotte, of Will—losses that had carved hollows in his soul.

Mandie was getting too close. Her kindness, her quiet strength, had seeped into those hollows, and he didn't know how to stop it.

"I don't know how to do this." He stared at the shadows. "To care for her and not be afraid every moment she's in danger."

He half-expected a nudge in his spirit, something telling him he was being ridiculous. But there was only silence.

And the weight of his fear remained.

CHAPTER 13

The morning sun had already crested over the eastern peaks when Mandie emerged from the house. The sky showed no hint of last night's storm. Only another bright summer day.

The men's voices sounded from the barn. All four brothers had started clearing out the burned debris right after the morning meal, but she'd stayed behind to clean the kitchen.

She'd not told the men she would be coming to help. And Enoch wouldn't be pleased to see her out here, of that she had no doubt.

Yet she couldn't sit idle while everyone else worked.

As she approached, the acrid smell of charred wood assaulted her senses. She breathed through her mouth, willing her stomach to settle. The barn looked even worse in daylight, with gaping holes in the roof and blackened timbers jutting up like broken teeth. The fire must have consumed nearly half the structure.

The clang of metal on charred wood sounded from within, and a pile of rubble sat outside to the left of the door.

James stepped through the open doorway, dragging a burned

log, his face streaked with soot. His white teeth flashed when he saw her. "Morning, Mrs. Beaumont. Come to lend a hand?"

She strode toward the doors he'd just exited. "I wouldn't miss it."

Inside the barn wasn't nearly as dark as usual. Having most of the ceiling gone certainly allowed in sunshine. Robert dipped a nod as he strode past her, carrying an armful of charred wood.

She returned a smile. The pieces he carried looked small enough for her to manage them. If the men could handle the dismantling, maybe she could help with the hauling.

"What are you doing?"

She turned toward the voice—Enoch's voice, of course—and had to search before spotting him up in the loft. What was left of the loft anyway.

His piercing blue eyes met hers, his scowl making his frustration plain. It seemed he'd removed his bandages already.

She kept her voice pleasant. "I'm here to help, like everyone else. Many hands make light work, as they say."

Enoch's jaw tightened, and he glanced at Thomas as if seeking support.

The younger brother shrugged, a small smile playing at the corners of his mouth. "She's right. We'll get this cleaned up faster with all of us working together."

Enoch gave a hard shake of his head. "A burned-out barn is no place for a lady."

She lifted her chin, meeting his gaze. "I'm no delicate flower. I can pull my weight, same as the rest of you."

For a moment, they stared at each other, a silent battle of wills. Then Enoch shook his head. The ghost of a smile tugging at his lips was starting to look familiar. "Fine. But take it slow and stop when you get tired." He gestured toward a smaller pile of rubble.

With a nod, Mandie set to work, her hands soon coated black as she hefted charred boards. The men kept an easy rhythm with their tasks, Thomas and James trading jibes as they labored. Even Robert joined in, his quiet strength evident as the brothers worked together.

When the sun climbed higher, hunger pangs gnawed at her stomach. She ignored them. If the men could work until midday without a break, she would too.

She should have eaten more at breakfast, but there was no help for it now.

Gritting her teeth, she hefted another sooty timber, the rough wood scraping her palms. Her stomach churned, and a wave of nausea washed over her. It was silly to think she would vomit from a little hard work and hunger. She could push through this.

But the queasiness only intensified, and a sour taste rose in the back of her throat. Her grip around the wood trembled.

Her stomach heaved. She was out of time.

Dropping the rubble, she sprinted out the barn door and around to the side, her vision tunneling as she fought to keep the nausea at bay.

She barely made it. Bracing herself against the rough wall, her insides retched, spewing out of her. Another surge came, her body shaking with the force of it. Then another.

She barely felt the hand gripping her elbow, holding her steady as she trembled with the force of her sickness.

Finally the spasms subsided. She could only stand there, bent over, as she caught her breath and searched for the strength to straighten. Her mind finally processed the reality that someone stood beside her, holding her elbow and rubbing her back.

Those strong hands. And the worn boots visible at the edge of her sight.

Mortification swept through her as she realized it was Enoch beside her, his large palm gentle on her back. Of all the people to witness her humiliation, it had to be him. She couldn't bear to meet his gaze, the disgust or pity in those piercing blue eyes.

But as she straightened, wiping her mouth with the back of her hand, a strange feeling pressed against her chest. Not nausea, but a churning apprehension, as if her body remembered something her mind could not. The sensation was so strong it nearly buckled her knees.

Closing her eyes, she tried to follow the feeling, to grasp at the elusive memory. A powder room materialized in her mind, but not the one at her home. At church, perhaps? And what had brought on this awful foreboding?

Was it Clayton, Nicholas's brother? He always had a way of making her skin crawl, his eyes following her with a predatory intensity.

Yet this was different, deeper than simple dislike or fear. As if some buried memory was trying to claw its way to the surface. A warning she couldn't quite grasp.

The memory slipped away like wisps of smoke, and she grabbed for it. Yet she couldn't…

Enoch's voice cut through her efforts. "Mandie? Are you all right?"

She opened her eyes to meet his. Worry creased his brow as he studied her.

She managed a nod. "I'm well now, truly. Something from breakfast just didn't agree with me. I'm ready to get back to work."

He shook his head, his expression brooking no argument. "Absolutely not. You're going back inside to rest. I'll carry you there myself if I have to."

She opened her mouth to protest, but the genuine concern in his eyes stopped her. Maybe he was right. Rest and food might be exactly what she needed to shake off this strange malaise.

With a sigh, she nodded. "I'll go inside and rest a bit."

Enoch's hand on her elbow tightened, as if he didn't quite trust her to make it back on her own. Then he released her, stepping back to give her space.

She turned toward the front of the barn, each step an effort as her body trembled with a bone-deep weariness that had nothing to do with the morning's labor. The feeling of foreboding still clung to her, an inexplicable dread that made her want to glance over her shoulder with every step.

As they emerged into the sunlight, the others paused in their work, concern etched on their faces. "What happened? Are you sick?"

Before she could respond, Enoch spoke up. "She's going inside to rest."

She managed a small smile for them. "I'll be all right. Just need a moment." Then she stumbled toward the house.

Enoch stayed at her side, matching her pace. His hand hovered near her elbow as if ready to catch her should she stumble.

She wanted to bristle at his coddling, to insist she was fine and could manage on her own. But the truth was, his solid presence beside her helped, easing some of the inexplicable dread that still coiled in her gut.

As they reached the porch steps, Enoch's hand came to rest on the small of her back, a gentle support as she climbed the stairs. The warmth of his touch seeped through her dress, and she leaned into it. Everything in her craved the solid reassurance of his strength.

And yet, even as she soaked in his comfort, the unease continued to churn within her. That half-remembered dread felt like a shadow she couldn't quite escape.

Whatever it was, she would have to face it. Soon.

CHAPTER 14

 $\mathcal{M}$ andie lay in the stillness of her room, the weight of her exhaustion pressing her into the mattress like a stone. Outside her window, the late-morning sun shone bright over the pines lining the yard, but the beauty seemed distant, unreachable.

She should be up and preparing food for the others to eat when they came in at midday. But she couldn't seem to make herself rise. What was this heaviness in her spirit? She no longer felt sick. Not after she came in and ate biscuits and sliced meat. She'd cleaned up the soot caked on her hands and dress, then sank into this bed.

She'd probably lain here an hour, and still she couldn't find the courage—or maybe energy?—to rise.

Footsteps sounded in the main room. The tread was heavy but measured, a stride she'd come to recognize over the past days.

Enoch. Her insides tightened. Was he coming to check on her? Or merely to prepare food for the men's midday meal? The thought of him entering her room, especially after seeing her make such a spectacle of herself outside…

The creaking of floorboards drew nearer, then paused outside her door. A gentle knock sounded, followed by Enoch's deep voice. "Mandie? May I open the door?"

She drew in a breath, trying to collect herself before answering. "Yes, come in." Her voice sounded thin, even to her own ears.

The door opened and Enoch stepped inside, his large frame filling the frame. His face and hands looked free of soot, and his collar and beard were wet. He must have washed up.

Worry still creased his forehead. "How are you feeling?" His gaze searched her face, as if trying to discern the truth for himself.

She managed a wan smile. "Better. Just tired." It wasn't the whole truth, but how could she explain the strange melancholy weighing her spirit? The unease she couldn't quite shake.

He nodded, but the furrow remained between his brows. "You gave us a scare out there. I thought..." He trailed off, shaking his head. "I'm glad you're all right."

Something in his tone, in the intensity of his gaze, made her heart ache. Enoch Balfour was not a man prone to sentimentality or coddling. Yet here he stood, his concern for her well-being evident in every line of his rugged face.

Maybe he would worry like this about any stranger put in his charge.

She pushed herself to sitting, the quilt pooling around her waist. "I'm sorry for causing concern. I don't know what came over me out there."

He took a step closer, then hesitated. "You have nothing to apologize for. You've been through a lot, and you're still recovering." His voice gentled. "I should have insisted you stay inside and rest from the start."

A wry smile tugged at her lips. "You did. I didn't listen."

His mouth quirked up at the corners. "You're right. I'm

learning that Mandie Beaumont is not a woman easily dissuaded from her course."

Something warm unfurled in her chest at his words, at the hint of admiration in his tone. She met his gaze, her smile growing. "I suppose I can be a bit…stubborn at times."

"A bit?" He raised his brows.

She let out a soft laugh. "Maybe more than a bit. But I prefer to think of it as determination."

"Call it what you will, it's a quality that will serve you well out here." His expression sobered. "Life on the frontier is not for the faint of heart."

"I'm beginning to see that." She'd never seen him so talkative, not without a purpose. Maybe he had something to say, or merely needed to rest and wanted conversation as he did so. She motioned to the chair near her bed. "Come and sit."

He hesitated, then stepped forward and sank into the seat. His large frame almost dwarfed the piece.

She cleared her throat. "How goes the work on the barn? I'm sorry I couldn't be of more help."

Enoch blinked, as if shaking himself from a spell. "Fine. We've cleared most of the debris. Tomorrow we'll start on repairs." He settled more into the chair. "But you needn't worry about that. Your only job is to rest and regain your strength."

She nodded, plucking at a loose thread on the quilt. The idea of more idle hours stretched before her, empty and echoing. She needed rest for her body to heal. But the inactivity chafed, leaving her too much time with her muddled thoughts.

And that sense of foreboding that lingered like a shadow at the edge of her mind.

She met Enoch's gaze, searching for words to voice her unease. "I know I need rest. But I can't seem to quiet my thoughts. Earlier, when I was ill, I had the strangest feeling. Like a memory trying to surface, but I couldn't quite grasp it."

His brow furrowed. "A memory? Of what?"

She shook her head. "Maybe not so much a memory as…a sensation. An impression." She closed her eyes, trying to recapture the fleeting images. "I remember being in a powder room, maybe at church."

She opened her eyes, but strained to find the feeling from before. "There was something awful." She met his gaze. "Something I had to get away from."

Enoch leaned forward, his elbows braced on his knees. "What? Was it a person?"

She frowned. "It's all so hazy. But the feeling was so strong. Like a warning I couldn't understand." She wrapped her arms around herself to fight against the chill inside her.

Enoch's jaw tightened. "Mandie, if someone hurt you, if that's why you left your home…" He trailed off, his hands curling into fists.

She shook her head. "I don't know." Her voice cracked, and she drew in a shuddering breath. *Was* that why she'd come west? Why she'd answered an advertisement for a mail-order bride? Had she actually intended to marry a man she'd never met in person? Or had that simply been the easiest way to escape whatever she'd feared in Savannah?

So many questions. They pressed in like a weight on her chest.

She rubbed the spot, and maybe that's what caused a strange fluttering sensation in her middle, like the brush of moth wings just below her ribs.

She sat up straighter and moved her hand to her belly where the motion had been.

Enoch leaned closer, his eyes sharpening. "What's wrong? Are you unwell again?"

She shook her head. "Not that. My insides are still unsettled, I suppose. I just felt this…flutter inside me."

His eyes searched hers, confusion and worry warring in their depths. "A flutter? Like sickness?"

She shook her head harder. "It's—"

The feeling came again, stronger this time. A definite flutter, like a fish darting just beneath the surface of a pond.

"Mandie. What's happening? What can I do?" Enoch's voice held a tinge of frustration. Or maybe desperation.

She forced out a slow breath and summoned a smile to calm him. "All is well. I likely just need rest."

He sat back in his chair, but his brows still gathered in a knot. "Mary Jenkins used to talk about fluttering in her belly when she was sick during her first months with…"

He trailed off, but of course he meant *with child*. One didn't speak of such things among mixed company. Especially not when she was lying in bed with him sitting in her bed chamber. Heat flushed up her neck. She should send him out.

But a new thought slid in to cover that one. Mary Jenkins felt fluttering in her middle when she was *with child*. Panic surged through her, but she tried not to let it show. Nicholas had been gone three years. There was no way she could be…

Right?

She'd not been with another man. Had she? Of course, she hadn't.

But this fear. This memory her body held of needing to escape. Had something happened?

A fragment of memory surfaced.

Not a clear picture, but a feeling—phantom hands gripping her arms, the press of a body against hers, the stench of cologne and spirits heavy in the air.

She squeezed her eyes shut as bile rose in her throat. She could barely breathe past the pressure on her chest.

"Mandie? Mandie, what's wrong?" Enoch's voice sounded in the distance, panic wrapping his tone.

She couldn't bear to face him. Not with the possibility…

But she had to.

She drew in a breath, forcing it to stay slow as she opened her eyes.

Enoch's blue eyes bored into hers, his hands gripping the arms of the chair as if to keep himself from reaching for her. "Tell me what's happening. Please."

She swallowed hard. She had to tell him something. That she'd found another memory. But as she opened her mouth to speak, emotion surged through her, choking off her voice. Tears stung her eyes and spilled down her cheeks before she could stop them.

Enoch made a low sound in his throat, almost a growl. He leaned forward, resting his hand on hers. "Mandie, please. Let me help." His grip wrapped around hers, warm, calloused. So strong.

The touch only unleashed more emotion. She shook her head, a sob catching in her throat. How could she voice the horrible suspicion taking root in her mind?

Dear God, is it possible? Could she be carrying a child conceived in violence? The thought made her stomach heave anew.

Enoch's grip tightened. "I'm going to send for the doctor. All right? Mandie?" So much worry weighted his voice.

She needed to say something. To calm him. It wasn't fair to worry him so. This was her weight to carry.

She sniffed and forced her breathing to slow as she met his gaze. "I'm all right. Truly. It might be good to bring a doctor though."

He held her gaze, and so much emotion swirled in his eyes, she could hardly read it all. Worry, for certain. Other things too, but she didn't have the energy to unpack everything.

He cleared his throat, and his voice rumbled deep when he spoke. "I'll send Robert now. Will you be all right until I come back?"

She nodded, the motion making tears drip from her chin to

her neck. "I'll be fine. Truly. I just...I think I'll try to sleep." She desperately needed time alone to process all this.

He looked torn, like he wasn't sure he could believe her.

She couldn't tell him her suspicion. What would he think?

At last, he gave her hand a small squeeze and pulled back as he stood. "I'll leave you alone then. Can I get you anything? Tea? Biscuits?" He paused for her answer, his height towering over the bed.

She shook her head. "Nothing, thank you."

He started toward the door but paused halfway. His gaze held hers for a long moment, his blue eyes filled with an intensity she couldn't name. "I'll be close by. If you need anything at all, just call for me."

She nodded, and he finally turned toward the door and slipped out.

She sank back against her pillow, her energy draining like water through a sieve.

Hot tears leaked from the corners of her eyes, and she finally let them come.

CHAPTER 15

*E*noch stood at the great room window, the blackness of night pressing in around him. Behind him, muted sounds came from his brothers—James and Thomas's chess pieces clacking against the board, Robert's occasional page turn. But they faded to a distant hum as his thoughts circled on the woman in the bed chamber down the hall.

Will's chamber. Though he rarely thought of the room that way anymore.

Mandie Beaumont had swept in and taken ownership of far too much around here. Including his thoughts.

He scrubbed a hand over his face, his calluses snagging in his beard. He'd been trying to keep from pacing for nearly a half hour now, ever since James returned with Doc Hansen in tow.

The doctor had disappeared down the hall to the bedchamber where Mandie rested, and Enoch had been tied in knots ever since.

Waiting. Worrying. His gut churning with possibilities he didn't want to consider.

"Enoch, come sit down." James's voice cut through the quiet, laced with a thread of exasperation. "Brooding won't make the doc finish any faster."

Enoch's jaw tightened, but he didn't turn from the window.

Robert spoke up, his tone gentler than James's. "Worrying won't change anything, Enoch. Mrs. Beaumont likely overdid it today. With some rest, she'll be fine."

Thomas snorted. "He's probably more worried that Mrs. Wang will give him what-for. He didn't take proper care of our guest."

The words were clearly meant to lighten the mood, to draw him out of his dark spiral of thoughts. But Enoch couldn't find it in himself to respond, couldn't muster even a halfhearted retort.

Not when his realization of Mandie's possible condition churned through his mind. After he'd made that comment about Mrs. Jenkins feeling a fluttering when she was with child… Mandie had reacted.

He'd not put the pieces together at the time, but now…

She'd said her husband died three years ago. Had she taken a lover in his absence? Was that the real reason she'd answered Will's mail-order bride advertisement?

The thought churned bile inside him. He couldn't reconcile the image of the kind, determined woman he'd come to know with such a scandalous act. But what other explanation could there be?

In truth, why would any beautiful, genteel widow leave her home and family to travel across the country and marry a complete stranger? The very idea seemed preposterous now that he thought about it.

The sound of a door opening jolted Enoch. He spun from the window to see Doc Hansen stepping into the main room, his weathered face unreadable.

Enoch strode forward to meet the man. "How is she?" The words came out harsher than he intended, almost a demand.

The doctor held up a hand, his expression calm. "Mrs. Beaumont will be fine with rest. But I'll let her share the details with you herself if she chooses."

His gut twisted tighter at the doctor's words. So there was something to tell. Something Mandie might choose to keep from him.

He gave a terse nod. "Thank you for coming."

"I'll be back to check on her in about a week." The doctor gathered his bag and headed for the door. "Send for me if anything changes before then."

As the door closed behind him, Enoch stood rooted to the spot, his mind racing. He had to know what the doctor had said. Had to know if his suspicions were correct.

Ignoring the questioning looks from his brothers, he strode down the hallway to Mandie's room. Her door stood ajar, lamplight spilling out into the dimness. He hesitated only a moment before rapping his knuckles softly against the wood.

"Come in." Her voice drifted out, soft and weary.

He pushed open the door and stepped inside. Shadows draped the room, the single lamp on the bedside table casting a soft glow over Mandie's pale face. She looked small and fragile propped against the pillows.

Too fragile.

His chest tightened at the sight of her so vulnerable, so unlike the vibrant, determined woman she'd proven to be.

"Are you..." His voice rasped, so he cleared his throat. "Are you well?"

She motioned to the chair beside the bed. "Please sit."

He hesitated, then crossed the room and lowered himself into the chair, the wood creaking beneath his weight. This close, he could see the faint tremble in her hands where they rested atop the quilt.

The urge to reach out and cover them with his own to offer

comfort and strength rose sharp and strong. He curled his fingers into his palms, holding himself in check.

Maybe now she would give him answers, explanations that would ease the knot in his gut. But would the truth only make things worse?

Mandie's dark eyes met his, a flicker of trepidation in their depths. Then her gaze moved away, settling on some distant point beyond his shoulder. "I...some of my memories returned today. Not all, but...enough to understand my condition."

His pulse pounded in his ears. "And?"

She drew in a shaking breath, her fingers gripping the quilt. "I believe my deceased husband's brother, he...he took advantage. Forced himself on me." Her voice cracked on the last words. "And the doctor confirmed that...that I am now with child."

A flash flood of emotions crashed through him. What man, what vile, filthy creature would commit such a heinous act? Against his brother's widow, no less.

Rage seared through him, hot and primal, urging him to violence against this monster. It took everything in him to keep from leaping to his feet. Demanding the man's name. He would make him pay. See him tortured until his last breath.

But Enoch forced himself to stay seated, to hear what Mandie was still saying.

Her face had grown paler than the white edging around the quilt. "I understand this isn't what you expected when you made your proposal. I'm aware the offer of marriage is likely no longer open to me."

She raised her chin, but he could see the tremor in it. "If you would allow me to impose on your hospitality a few more days, until I regain my strength, I would be most grateful. Then I'll be on my way."

Her words pierced through the red haze of his fury, dousing

it like icy water. She thought he would rescind his proposal? Turn her out because of the vile acts of another?

"No." The word burst from him, almost too loud.

She flinched, and he took in a breath, then forced himself to speak more gently. "I am so, *so* sorry that happened to you, Mandie." His voice broke midway through that sentence, but he pressed on. "Sorrier than I can say. If you haven't already brought the man to justice, I will gladly do so myself."

He leaned forward to catch her gaze, willing her to see the sincerity in his. "As for the rest, my offer still stands. I would never hold against you something so awful done *to* you. You're not to blame in the slightest. And the child..." His throat tightened. "I was raised to believe a child is a blessing from God. A gift to celebrate. To protect and cherish. I'd be honored to do so. For you both."

Mandie stared at him, her dark eyes wide and shimmering with unshed tears. "You can't mean that." Her voice came out as little more than a whisper. "A child born from such circumstances—"

"Is innocent." He cut her off before she could finish the thought.

He reached out and took her hand in his. Such a small, delicate hand against his roughened palm. "This babe has done nothing wrong. And neither have you."

A single tear slipped down her cheek, and she dashed it away with her free hand. "But the scandal, the shame it would bring on your family...on you. How can I ask you to bear that?"

He tightened his grip on her fingers, willing her to feel his conviction. "You're not asking. I am." He held her gaze, letting her see the truth in his eyes. "I'm strong enough to help. To face this with you." He infused his tone with a bit of that strength. "Please let me."

Mandie's eyes searched his for a long moment. At last, she drew in a shuddering breath, her fingers tightening around his.

"I don't know what to say." Her voice trembled, thick with emotion. "Your kindness, your generosity...it's more than I could have hoped for."

He squeezed her hand, a gentle pressure. "You don't have to say anything. Just know that my offer comes with no conditions, no expectations. I want to help in whatever way I can."

She nodded, another tear slipping free to trail down her cheek. "Thank you, Enoch. Truly. I...I don't know if I can accept. Not yet. It's so much to take in." Her free hand drifted to her middle, resting there. "But knowing I have a choice, that I'm not alone in this...it means more than you can know."

His chest tightened at the vulnerability, the tentative hope in her eyes. He wanted to pull her into his arms, to shelter her from all the cruelties and hurts the world had inflicted. But he held himself in check.

She'd had too many choices stripped away. He wouldn't pressure her now.

"You have all the time you need." He kept his voice as soothing as his rough tone could manage. "And whatever you decide, you have a place here, for as long as you need it." With a final gentle squeeze, he released her hand and sat back. "I'll let you sleep. Can I bring you anything?"

She shook her head. "No. Thank you." She hesitated. "Only..."

He leaned forward again. "Yes?"

"I...can we not tell your brothers? Yet. About the babe, I mean. I just... I want to come to terms with it myself first."

That tightness pulled in his chest again. How hard it must be to face all this in such a wave. "Of course. When you're ready. I'll tell them you merely need rest for now. They're nosy buzzards, but they won't push." They wouldn't push *her* at least. They'd nag at Enoch until he put an end to it.

A hint of a weary smile curved her lips. "Thank you."

He stood and moved away from her bed. "Call out if you need anything."

She nodded. "I will."

As he reached the door, her voice drifted to him. "Good night, Enoch."

With his hand on the knob, he glanced back at her. "Good night, Mandie."

Something about those words, the simple sentiment using her given name, felt far too intimate for his heart. He'd best do a better job of shoring it up, or he'd be hurting once again when he lost this woman too.

CHAPTER 16

She couldn't spend another moment wallowing in her tears.

Not when there was so much to do. Not when Mandie could help in at least a small way by preparing meals for these men who'd taken her in with such kindness. Enoch especially.

As the first blush of dawn showed outside the window, she pushed herself from the bed, ignoring the lingering ache in her head. She dressed quickly, then pinned her hair into a chignon at the nape of her neck. A glance in the mirror showed her face still bore traces of the previous day's tears. Hopefully that would fade once she got moving.

The house remained quiet as she stepped softly down the hall and into the kitchen. The cookstove was already lit with the coffeepot on the surface, which meant at least one other person was up. A check inside the pot showed the water just starting to boil.

She set to work pulling out the biscuits Bea had made the morning she left. They were starting to grow hard, but would hopefully still be fresh enough to serve. To go with them? Would the men mind fried ham and eggs again like she'd prepared yesterday? She had no idea how to prepare pastries, and she'd not found potatoes anywhere.

"You're up early."

She jumped at the deep voice behind her. Enoch.

She turned to find him standing in the kitchen doorway, his broad shoulders filling the frame. The morning light filtering through the small window cast his rugged features in sharp relief, highlighting the angles of his jaw beneath his beard.

"I wanted to get breakfast started." She kept her voice low. The others might still be sleeping.

His blue eyes searched her face, concern etching lines around them. "How are you feeling?"

She summoned a smile, hoping it reached her eyes. "Better. Truly. I needed the rest yesterday, but I can't spend all day in bed again. Not when there's so much to be done."

He stepped closer, his large frame filling the small kitchen. Even with the island between them, his presence surrounded her. "You've been through a lot, Mandie. No one expects you to push yourself before you're ready."

His use of her given name, the gentleness in his tone, sent a flutter through her middle. How was it that this man she barely knew could both unsettle and comfort her with a few simple words?

She lifted her chin. "I *am* ready. Helping, even in small ways, will make me feel more myself again."

He held her gaze a moment longer, then inclined his head. "All right. But promise you'll stop if it's too much."

"I will." She turned back to the work counter to begin slicing ham. Anything to hide the effect his nearness had on her composure.

He moved to the stove to check the coffeepot, and she tried not to notice the way his shoulders strained against his shirt, or the fluid grace of his movements despite his size. His hair and beard curled damp around his face, like he'd just washed up.

The scent of his soap drifted to her, clean and masculine, mingling with the aroma of woodsmoke. She focused on the ham, the rasp of the knife against the cutting board, and tried to ignore the awareness prickling along her skin.

He reached for the mugs hanging on pegs by the window. "The others will be in soon. They'll be glad for a hot meal."

Mandie nodded, focusing on the steady rhythm of her knife against the cutting board. "I hope this will do. I'm afraid my culinary skills are a bit lacking compared to Bea's."

Enoch's low chuckle sent a shiver down her spine. "I reckon anything you make will be a sight better than what we'd rustle up on our own."

She glanced over her shoulder, a smile tugging at her lips. "I'll bet the four of you could handle things." They likely possessed any number of skills the dandies back east couldn't manage.

"You'd be surprised. Thomas once tried to make hoecakes and nearly set the kitchen ablaze."

Mandie laughed, the sound feeling rusty and unfamiliar in her throat. "I'll do my best to keep from a similar fate."

Enoch's gaze warmed, a glint of humor softening the blue. "Thank you for saving us from ourselves."

At last, he turned and left the room, steaming cup in hand.

She let out a long breath. When would her body stop reacting to his every word and look?

Soon the scent of frying ham and eggs filled the kitchen, and she could hear the men's voices drifting in from the other room as they gathered for the morning meal.

She arranged the food on platters, then gathered her courage and carried them and the coffeepot out to the dining room. The brothers were all seated around the table, their conversation halting as she entered.

"Good morning." She set the platters in the center of the

table, trying not to feel self-conscious under their gazes. "I hope you're hungry."

"Famished." Thomas eyed the ham with undisguised eagerness. "This looks a right sight better than what Enoch would have made."

Enoch shot his brother a glare as he took the coffeepot from her with one hand and pulled out her chair for her with the other. "You're not wrong about that, but at least I haven't set fire to the kitchen yet."

It didn't feel right letting Enoch pour the coffee while she sat, but it felt less proper to argue with him for the task. So she lowered herself and allowed him to push in her chair.

Robert cleared his throat. "We're most grateful for the meal, Mrs. Beaumont. Your efforts are appreciated." He shot Thomas a quelling look.

Mandie smiled, relaxing a bit as she smoothed her napkin in her lap. "It's the least I can do after all your kindness. And please, call me Mandie. *Mrs. Beaumont* feels far too formal."

After Enoch poured the coffee and took his seat, they all bowed for James to say a prayer. As he asked God's blessing on the food, she sent up her own petition. *Help me know what to do, Lord. Send guidance.*

As soon as they spoke the *amen*, the men filled their plates and tucked in. Mandie nibbled at her food, her stomach still unsettled. She had no idea now if it was from all the unrest in her spirit, or from the effects of the new life growing inside her.

A child.

She still couldn't fathom that fact. But she was coming to think of the babe as part of herself.

Conversation flowed around her, the brothers discussing the day's tasks.

"We need to get the order in for the barn wood soon." Robert glanced around at Enoch.

"You want to go do that today while we cut new poles for the supports?" Enoch took a drink of his coffee. "You can check the telegraph office again while you're there, see if a reply came for Mandie."

"And then swing by the Jenkins place on your way back," Thomas added. "Check if Bea's ready to come home."

Robert gave a quick nod. "I'll take care of it."

Mandie's heart skipped at the mention of a possible reply from her parents. She'd nearly forgotten about the telegram in the upheaval of yesterday's revelations. What would they say? How much did they know? Would they be worried sick over her disappearance? Her injury?

She needed to tell them about the babe, but she couldn't bear the thought of them learning the truth of her situation through an impersonal wire. She should compose a proper letter, break the news gently, and in full sentences. But what could she possibly say to explain all that had transpired?

What would they do when they learned Clayton had done the unthinkable? Her parents had always thought so highly of him, approving of his intentions toward her even before she came out of mourning. The scandal would be devastating, especially with Papa's bid for mayor coming up.

Enoch's deep voice pulled her from her spiraling thoughts. "We'll fell the logs for the poles this morning, then haul and peel them." He glanced at James and Thomas. "If we push, we might get them set today too."

The other two nodded, easy communication among men who knew each other so well. What would it be like to be a part of a family like this? To belong as one of them?

The forbidden thought crept in before she could stop it. If she accepted Enoch's proposal, this could be her family. These men, this land, could be her home.

She pushed the idea away. England would be her home. Enoch said he would have to go there. Besides, this decision was too big to be swayed by emotion.

Better to focus on something she could look forward to... Bea would return by tonight.

The prospect of having the older woman's steady presence and wisdom back in the house eased some of the tension in Mandie's shoulders. And her cooking skills. Mandie would pay far better attention to Bea's recipes from here on out.

She'd never realized how hard it was to cook a full breakfast and dinner, as well as have cold food set out at midday. Had preparing food been easier in Savannah, where breads and meats could be bought freshly baked? Maybe, but their cooks had also made much fancier meals than she or even Bea had turned out here, where every detail had to be accomplished from scratch.

As the meal concluded, the men rose to begin their work. Each thanked her for the meal, though it was only fried ham, leftover biscuits, and eggs. Barely hearty enough for all the work they'd be doing.

Enoch paused as she stood to collect the dishes. "I can bring in more water for you before we head out, if you need it for cleaning up."

She sent him a small smile. "That would be much appreciated, thank you."

He nodded, his gaze lingering on her face a moment longer before he turned and strode out the door.

Mandie busied herself clearing the table, doing her best not to dwell on the way her pulse quickened at his nearness, at the gentle timbre of his voice when he spoke to her.

It was only natural to feel drawn to his strength and steadiness in the midst of her own upheaval. But she couldn't let herself depend on him too much, couldn't let gratitude blur into something more dangerous.

By the time he returned with the pail of water, she had the dishes neatly stacked in the kitchen and the table wiped down. He set the bucket in the sink, then hesitated.

"If you need anything, just call out. I'll be working close by today."

"I'll be fine. Truly." She looked up at him, willing confidence into her voice. "I may be a bit slower at the chores than Bea, but I'm capable."

That ghost of a smile touched his lips, there and gone. "I don't doubt that." His eyes held hers a second longer. Then he gave a short nod and turned for the door. "That mare will likely foal today or tomorrow, so I'll be within shouting distance if you need me."

A mare due to foal… Wasn't that the one Enoch nearly died saving in the fire?

Thought of the fire spurred something else she'd forgotten.

Enoch was nearly out of the kitchen when she called out. "Wait, Enoch. Your burns. I can see that your head and neck are healing, but the rest…I haven't checked them since that first night."

He paused and half-turned back. "It's all right. I've been putting the salve on. James says they look to be healing well."

Disappointment pricked through her. Of course his brothers would be tending to him. He didn't need her help. "That's good. I'm glad they're improving."

With that, he ducked out the door, leaving her alone with the morning sunlight and a counter stacked with dirty dishes.

She let out a slow breath and set to work, plunging her hands into the warm, soapy water. At least she had work to distract her from all the questions churning inside.

CHAPTER 17

The sun had just begun to sink behind the mountains, casting long shadows across the ranch, as Robert rode in alone. Enoch's chest tightened as he watched from the barn doorway where he, James, and Thomas were still working.

No Mrs. Wang.

He studied his brother's face as he reined in his horse in front of Enoch. "She wasn't ready to come yet?" Maybe the birth had taken longer than usual, and Mrs. Wang felt the need to stay another day until the mother was up on her feet.

Robert shook his head, then dismounted. "There was trouble in the birthing. Mary's not able to get up much, and the babe's small, not eating well yet." He turned to face Enoch, and the weariness lining his eyes spoke of the journey. "Mrs. Wang said she'll likely need to stay with them another week at least."

A week.

Enoch exhaled slowly, measuring his response. Another week without Mrs. Wang's steady presence meant another week with Mandie handling the household alone. She was more than capable. He had no doubt about that. But she needed rest.

And he had a feeling she'd appreciate having another woman

to talk through her condition with. Especially someone experienced in helping with births like Mrs. Wang. For some reason, God had never seen fit to give the Wangs their own children, but she'd assisted with at least a dozen birthings through the years, including Robert's and Thomas's deliveries, if he remembered right.

A week.

He'd have to do his best to fill in the gap with Mandie, though he was a poor second choice to their wonderful housekeeper.

He eyed his brother again. "What about a telegram?" News from her parents would surely cheer Mandie's spirits.

Robert shook his head again, this time with a grimace. "Nothing. I did get the wood ordered though."

Enoch's jaw tightened. He was still moving slowly from the burns. And then on top of it, no Mrs. Wang and no word from Mandie's parents. The Lord certainly wasn't making things easy.

"How's she been?" Robert lowered his voice as he glanced toward the house.

"Managing." Enoch turned to walk beside his brother and the mount into the barn. "Better than managing, truth be told. You wouldn't know she wasn't raised to this life."

Robert's gaze turned to scan the interior of the barn where Thomas and James fitted one of the final poles in the ground beside the far wall. "You boys got a lot done today."

"Enoch's a hard taskmaster." Thomas kept his focus on the pole he held. "Didn't even let us stop for a nap."

Enoch shook his head. "There's only one more to set after that one." He eyed Robert. "Think you could help while I see if Mandie needs any help with the food? I don't want her overdoing." He should have gone in a half hour ago to check on her, but it took three of them to raise one of these tree trunks and secure it to the beams at the top.

Robert nodded and turned to unfasten the saddle from his mount. "Go on."

Enoch strode to the house, keeping himself to a walk, though part of him wanted to sprint. When he opened the door, the smell of something savory greeted him—a rich, hearty aroma that made his stomach growl in anticipation. He'd not realized how hungry he was.

He found Mandie at the stove, her back to him, hair pinned up with a few tendrils escaping to curl against her neck. The sight of her there, stirring the pot, struck him with an odd feeling of rightness that tightened his chest. As much as he needed her to stay, to agree to be his wife for the sake of the duchy, she stirred too much inside him.

He couldn't let all these feelings come alive. Couldn't let his heart get attached. But he couldn't turn her out. Where else could she go? Did she have another choice? Did he?

He cleared his throat to announce his presence as he stepped into the kitchen. "Smells good."

She startled slightly, turning to face him. "I didn't hear you come in." A smile curved her lips, though it didn't quite reach her eyes. "I'm trying to make a stew."

"I think you mastered it." He moved closer, fighting the urge to reach out and brush back a tendril of damp hair that had wrapped nearly to her chin. "Robert's here."

Her eyes widened with hope. "And Mrs. Wang?"

He shook his head. "She needs to stay another week with the family." Enoch watched the hope fade from Mandie's eyes, replaced by something that looked like resignation. "The mother's having trouble recovering, and the baby isn't eating well."

"Oh." Mandie turned back to the stew, giving it another stir. "Of course she must stay. They need her more than we do."

But he could see the slight slump of her shoulders, the way her hands tightened on the wooden spoon. He stepped closer, though careful to keep a little distance.

"And…was there any word from my parents?" Her question came softly, her back still to him.

Enoch hesitated. If only he had better news. "I'm afraid not. Robert did check."

Her shoulders tensed, then relaxed with deliberate control. "I see. They're likely just… busy."

The silence stretched between them, broken only by the bubbling of the stew and the crackle of the fire.

He took another step closer. "How can I help with the food?"

"It's nearly ready." She glanced up at him. "I hope you're not getting tired of biscuits. There's not any other kind of bread, and I didn't know what else…" A flash of something like worry —or maybe even panic—lit her gaze, then disappeared as she turned back to the pot.

Realization slipped through him. She may not know how to make bread or biscuits. He'd not thought about the fact that Mrs. Wang had all her recipes stored in the rich recesses of her mind. Mandie likely knew little more about cooking than him. Less even, for had she ever been without a paid cook?

He kept his voice gentle. "Mrs. Wang's biscuits are good enough to eat every meal for a week. I don't know how she makes them, and I doubt she has the recipe written down anywhere. I do know how to make her skillet cornbread though. I used to help her every so often, and that one was easy enough for me to handle on my own. I can show you whenever you like."

"Thank you." She glanced at him, gratitude flickering across her features. "Maybe tomorrow morning?"

They must be almost out of biscuits then. He nodded and sent a smile. "Perfect. That'd go nice with ham. We can start beans soaking tonight so they can cook tomorrow for the evening meal. Beans and cornbread is James's favorite meal."

Relief flooded her expression. "I'd appreciate that. I'd hate to disappoint everyone."

"You haven't disappointed anyone." So very much the opposite. "You've been remarkable."

She ducked her head at the compliment, and something warm flickered in his chest. He tamped it down. His job was to protect her, not fall for her.

He moved to the cupboard, pulling down plates and cutlery. "I'll set the table." Best he keep busy.

By the time his brothers came in from the barn and washed, Mandie had ladled stew into all the bowls and set them out on the table. She'd also positioned flowers in the middle, though he had no idea when she'd gathered them.

The entire scene looked…different. Better. She might not know all the frontier cooking skills, but she brought refinement to their table.

Once his brothers settled and James spoke the blessing, his brothers filled the silence with their usual conversation. Thomas and James squabbled about who'd felled the most trees, then Robert shared news from town. Not much new since he'd gone to take the telegram two days before.

Enoch watched Mandie throughout the meal, and she appeared to relax as conversation flowed around her, though her eyes still held that shadow of worry.

After the dishes were cleared and washed—he and his brothers did that part, despite Mandie's protests—Thomas and James set up the chessboard as they did most evenings, while Robert settled into his favorite chair with a dog-eared book. Enoch attempted to do the same with his Bible, though he kept an eye on Mandie as she sank onto one of the upholstered chairs.

The familiar rhythm of their evening routine settled over the house, but Mandie seemed to hover at its edges, not quite finding her place.

"Care to join us for a game?" Thomas gestured to the chess pieces.

"Oh, I..." Mandie hesitated. "I've never really played chess."

"I could teach you." Thomas flashed one of his smiles that always won Mrs. Wang over. "It's not as complicated as it looks."

That charm didn't work as well on Mandie though. "Thank you, but perhaps another time." She folded her hands in her lap, her gaze drifting toward the window where darkness was gathering.

Enoch recognized that restless look. He felt it himself sometimes when the walls of the house pressed in too close, when his thoughts grew too loud.

He set his Bible on the side table and stood. "I need to check on the mare." He kept his voice casual as he looked to Mandie. "Would you like to come along? Might be nice to get outside when it's cooler."

Relief flickered across her face. "I'd like that."

He grabbed a lantern from near the door, lit it from the one on the corner table, then handed Mandie her shawl from the peg. "You might need this. The evenings can get chilly when we're nearing autumn."

The soft wool settled over her shoulders as she wrapped it around herself. She looked so at home in that moment, preparing to walk with him under the starlight.

He swallowed and turned to open the door, allowing her to pass first.

The evening had cooled considerably, the mountain air crisp against his skin as they crossed the yard toward the stable. Stars were beginning to prick the darkening sky, and a sliver of moon hung above the mountains.

Beside him, Mandie drew a deep breath, her shoulders lowering as tension visibly drained from her frame. "It's beautiful here." Her voice came out soft, almost reverent. "So vast."

"Different from Savannah, I imagine."

"Very." She glanced at him. "Though both have their own kind of beauty."

The lantern light caught the angles of her face, softening them. She was certainly the most beautiful woman he'd ever met, but he was doing his best to ignore that fact.

Forcing his focus ahead, he held the barn door open for her, and the familiar smells of hay and horses greeted them as they entered. At least most of the smoky scent was gone now.

"She's here at the front." He motioned toward the mare in the first stall, and Mandie moved that direction. "This is Willow."

Willow nickered as they approached, stretching her neck over the stall door. Her coat glistened. Was that sweat?

He reached to run his hand down the mare's neck. Not sweat, just her thin summer coat in the lantern light. He'd been watching for days now for any sign of early labor—pacing, sweating, nipping at her flanks. So far, only a bit of leaking milk showed that her time was imminent.

Mandie stroked the mare's jaw and muzzle, clearly comfortable with horses. "She's lovely."

Willow nudged Mandie's palm, and her white teeth flashed in a smile—the first he'd seen from her all evening. Something in his chest eased at the sight.

"Hello, beautiful girl," she murmured, stroking the mare with those long, delicate fingers. "Are you going to be a mother soon?"

Enoch tore his gaze away from the pair and slipped into the stall, then moved down the mare's side to check her flanks and udder. More dried milk on her hind legs. Her sides weren't as rounded either, which meant the baby had moved into the birth canal.

"When will her foal come?"

He stepped back to study the mare as a whole. "Tonight mayhap. Tomorrow night at the latest."

Mandie stroked the mare's neck. "Will she need help?"

"Most times they don't." Enoch moved close again to run a

hand down Willow's sleek shoulder. "But sometimes there's trouble. I usually sleep out here when they're this close."

Which brought his dilemma into sharp focus. Normally, he'd bed down in the straw nearby so he would hear when the mare started to get restless.

But with Mandie in the house, he hesitated. What if she woke in the night and needed something? Or cried out with nightmares stirred by her recent memories? He knew well enough how trauma could send dark dreams slithering through the night.

"You don't have to stay out here all night." Mandie stroked Willow's jaw in a steady rhythm. "I'd be happy to take a turn watching her."

Mandie sleep in the barn? Lose sleep from waking to check on the mare? Not a chance.

But as he studied Mandie's face in the lantern light. The softness there was genuine, not the polite mask she sometimes wore around the house. Here with the animals, she seemed more at ease.

"I appreciate the offer." He kept his voice low to avoid startling the mare. "But I couldn't ask that of you."

"You didn't ask. I offered." Her eyes met his with that determination he'd half-learned to expect by now.

He held in a sigh. He'd not yet successfully managed to stop her when she took on this expression.

Perhaps having a task, something to focus on beyond her own troubles, would help her. He could cling to that thought, for he didn't seem to have another choice.

He motioned for them to step out of the stall and fastened the latch behind them. Then he led her to the stall next to Willow's. "I've brought in blankets, and I'll already have a lantern lit. The cracks between boards are wide enough you can easily see her if she starts to pace or sounds like she's in pain."

She nodded. "And you'll wake me up around two o'clock?"

She eyed him, probably realizing he might try to keep from committing.

This time, he did let his sigh come. "If you're certain. And if she hasn't already foaled."

Mandie straightened. "If the baby comes before, please wake me. I'd so love to see the birth."

The hope glimmering in her eyes, excitement even, nearly tugged a smile from him. But he responded with the same begrudging answer. "If you're certain."

Yet as they turned back toward the house, he couldn't keep the smile in. This woman with all her genteel ways and city raising just might learn to fit in this mountain country after all.

CHAPTER 18

Enoch jolted awake, flinching a bit as his healing wounds pulled. Darkness surrounded him, so why had he awakened? His bed… That's right, he was in the barn.

Willow.

He peered between the boards into her stall.

The mare was pacing, her tail swishing up and down. She paused to paw at the straw, then let out a low nicker.

It was time.

He watched a few minutes longer, just to gauge where she was in the process. Had her waters broken yet? At that point, she wouldn't be able to stop her laboring. But if he brought Mandie too soon, Willow might worry about the spectators and slow the birthing down.

In the dim light from the lantern he'd left burning, he could see the sheen of sweat on her flanks, the tension in her muscles as she paced.

Then finally, she lifted her tail, and a gush of fluid splashed onto the straw. That had to be it.

As Willow dropped to the ground with a groan, he pushed to his feet and slipped out of the barn.

Things could happen quickly now, and he hated for Mandie to miss any part. Seeing new life come into the world was, indeed, special.

When he stepped into the house, the place lay dark and still, the embers of the fire casting a faint glow in the main room. He moved quietly down the hall and paused at Mandie's door so he could knock.

"Mandie?" He kept his voice low. "The foal's coming now."

A rustle of movement came from within, then a moment later, the door opened. Mandie stood before him, a shawl thrown around the same dress she'd been wearing before bed. Some of her dark hair pulled loose from her braid, framing her beautiful face in a way that made him want to pull her close.

Her eyes glimmered with excitement. "Is everything all right?"

"So far." He stepped back to allow her passage. "But we should hurry. She's already down."

She strode ahead of him, and he had to lengthen his steps to keep up. He followed her out the door and across the yard, then grabbed the barn door for her as they both slipped inside.

Mandie slowed inside the barn and crept forward to stand outside the opening to Willow's stall.

The mare lay on the ground still, but faced a different direction than when he'd left her. This angle gave them a somewhat awkward view of her abdomen, with all four feet facing toward them as the mare lay flat and grunted. She was pushing through a pain, and a glimmer of white appeared by her tail.

He moved up beside Mandie and pointed to the spot as he kept his voice low. "There it is."

She jumped beside him, as though she'd not expected him to speak. When she sent a quick look up at him, he couldn't help a grin.

A grunt from the stall pulled their attention back to Willow.

The mare was obviously straining, the rippling muscles easily seen where sweat plastered her thick coat.

He kept focus on that white bubble at the horse's tail, larger now than before. The white glimmer expanded, inch by painful inch. One end darkened, and a tiny black hoof broke through the slippery bubble.

Mandie gasped beside him, the sound almost drowned out by Willow's heavy breathing. "Is that...a foot?" Her whisper held a tremor of awe.

Enoch nodded, his chest tight with anticipation. "The front feet come first, then the nose."

Tension in the air thickened as they waited for the next hoof. And waited.

At least a minute must have passed since their first view of the foot, but no more activity. His eye tracked back to the mare, up to her shoulder. Willow bobbed her head against the stall floor, then raised it, tucking her chin tight to her chest. Veins rose across her shoulders and abdomen. Everything in the horse fought to expel this new life.

Mandie grabbed his arm. "Something's wrong." Panic laced her voice. "We have to do something."

He covered her hand with his own to steady them both. "She's all right."

Her gaze flicked to him, filled with concern. "The baby's not moving." Her words edged with panic. "What if it's twisted inside?" Her hand gripped even tighter around his arm—a touch of warmth he hadn't realized he craved until now.

He kept his voice low, hopefully calm enough to soothe both females. "It's just the shoulders. That part's always tricky. Once they're through, you'll see—the little one will start moving."

Mandie turned her gaze forward again and tensed as the mare gave an awful groan and pressed flat against the ground. With a whoosh, the foal spewed halfway out, the white bubble pulling away to reveal a tiny brown head. From ears to shoulders was still covered with white though.

"Oh." Mandie breathed the sound, probably not realizing she'd spoken.

He couldn't help watching the woman instead of the horse. In the lanternlight, with such wonder on her face, her beauty stole his breath. Made his chest ache too much to let in air.

Mandie's fingers dug into his arm, forcing his focus back to the mare and foal. "Is he breathing?"

Enoch studied the foal. The nostrils flared the slightest bit. Good.

Before he could reassure Mandie, Willow moved. With a final massive effort, the horse surged to her feet, and the rest of the foal slipped out onto the straw, tearing away the white bubble with a tangle of spindly legs.

For one heart-stopping moment, the babe lay motionless. *Please, Lord.*

Then the little chest heaved, and the foal sneezed, shaking its head as it drew in gulps of air. Willow turned and gave a soft nicker as she began licking the birthing fluids from her baby's face.

Mandie sagged against Enoch, her head dropping to his good shoulder as she let out a tremulous sigh. "Oh, thank God. I was so afraid..."

He wrapped an arm around her waist to steady her. Had she been thinking about the fact that she'd be giving birth, too, in a few months? Seeing Willow's pain must surely have raised all kinds of worries. He'd been a thoughtless cad, suggesting she be here for this birthing.

But then she let out a tremulous sigh, her body shifting against him. "That was...incredible." Her voice wavered with emotion. "I've never seen anything so amazing."

Enoch nodded, his throat tight. No matter how many times he witnessed this miracle, it never failed to move him.

With Mandie pressed warm against his side, her scent surrounding him, the moment seemed to stretch and suspend. He didn't want to move, didn't want to risk shattering this fragile connection growing between them. And yet as her movement spiked pain in his burned skin, he knew they would only cause each other heartache. Could either of them endure more?

The foal lifted its head, blinking in the dim light. Those long legs splayed out in all directions as it tried to coordinate them. Willow continued her licking, cleaning her baby, and getting its blood flowing.

"It's a filly." Enoch grinned. "A strong one too, by the looks of her."

Mandie sighed, and some of the tension drained from her body as she leaned into him. "She's perfect."

Perfect. The word echoed in his mind as he looked down at Mandie, her face soft with wonder and joy. The urge to pull her closer, to press his lips to hers, nearly overwhelmed him.

And when she lifted her face to look up at him...he could no longer stop himself.

He raised his free hand to cup her cheek, his thumb brushing the silken skin.

Her eyes widened, but she didn't pull away. Instead, her lips parted slightly, an invitation he couldn't resist.

Slowly, giving her time to turn away, he lowered his head. When his lips met hers, all rational thought fled.

Her mouth was soft and warm, molding perfectly to his. A small sound escaped her, somewhere between a sigh and a whimper, and it nearly undid him.

He deepened the kiss, his hand sliding into her hair to cradle the back of her head. She tasted of sweetness and hope. The water his parched body had been craving.

Her fingers curled into his shirt, holding him close as she

returned the kiss with a tentative passion that set his blood on fire.

A lifetime could have passed and he would have been happy to stay in this place. Nothing existed beyond the feel of Mandie in his arms, the rightness of her body pressed to his.

A snort from the stall broke the spell.

Mandie pulled back, her breath coming in soft pants. Her eyes were wide and dark in the lantern light, her lips kiss-swollen and tempting.

He shouldn't have done that. Should he?

He'd asked her to marry him. She might be his in truth one day soon.

But he didn't *want* a connection with her. Did he? He'd promised himself he wouldn't let his heart grow attached. He wouldn't leave himself vulnerable.

So he forced himself to pull back. To put space between them. "I'm sorry. I shouldn't have…" His back throbbed along with his head.

She ducked her chin and shook her head, turning back to the mare and foal. "It was just the excitement of the moment."

A lie. And his body hummed with confirmation of that fact.

This woman stirred him like no other ever had. Not even Charlotte. Looking back, he'd been drawn as much to Charlotte's family as to her. The idea of having parents in his life again. A complete unit, not broken and scattered like his own.

But Mandie.

Everything about this woman drew him. That kiss. Her beauty. Her determination. Her gentleness.

He took a step back, forcing himself to turn away. He should find the cloths he'd brought out to help dry the foal.

Best he get to work so his heart didn't lead him down another painful trail.

CHAPTER 19

Mandie took another bite of her boiled oats as the brothers' conversation drifted around her. These had turned out better than she'd expected.

Yesterday—the morning after Willow's foaling—she'd come into the kitchen to find a hot skillet of cornbread cooling on the back of the stove, a pot of beans soaking in cold water, and a note on the counter from Enoch. Rather, a recipe, written in his bold hand, with instructions on how to make the cornbread herself and how to cook the beans.

Last evening, she'd found another note with instructions on boiling oats, which he mentioned in the postscript at the bottom of the recipe was a favorite of his brothers too.

He'd avoided speaking to her though, unless absolutely necessary. And then, he wouldn't look at her.

Had she done something wrong in that kiss? Responded too fervently? The thought made her neck heat, and she took another bite of her oats.

James's voice cut through her thoughts. "Enoch, you said something about checking on the herd in the north pasture?"

Enoch cleared his throat. "I'll ride out after breakfast. Check on that herd of cattle we moved last week."

Mandie's heart leapt. Did she dare ask? She so desperately needed air, space, a chance to clear her head. Being cooped up in the house with only her thoughts was driving her batty.

She lifted her gaze to his, trying to read the guarded expression in those piercing blue eyes.

"Could I...could I come with you?" The words tumbled out before she could second-guess herself. "I would love some fresh air."

Enoch's fork paused halfway to his mouth, his gaze snapping to hers. Surprise flicked across his face. "I don't know if that's a good idea."

Mandie swallowed hard, her throat dry. "Please. I'm feeling cooped up and restless. I promise I won't be any trouble."

Enoch's jaw tightened, and for a moment, he looked like he would refuse. But then he sighed, setting down his fork. "All right. But we'll need to leave soon if we want to be back before dark."

Relief washed through her, followed by a flutter of anticipation. A day alone with Enoch, away from the tension of the house... It would either be awkward or wonderful. Probably both.

She quickly finished her breakfast and started to gather the used dishes from the table.

Robert stood and waved her away. "My turn for clean-up today. You go get ready." He sent a look Enoch's way. "If I know my brother, he'll be ready to ride out in a few minutes."

Enoch didn't voice a response, and she didn't check his expression, just thanked Robert and went to change into her split skirt and boots.

As she braided her hair tightly, she caught sight of her reflection in the small mirror. Her cheeks were flushed, her eyes bright. She looked...excited. Happy, even.

Somehow, Enoch already had two horses saddled and waiting in front of the house when she stepped outside.

He didn't look at her as she descended from the porch, simply turned to the sorrel and moved around to her side. "This is Rosie. She taught Thomas how to ride, so she should be gentle enough."

In other words, he assumed she would be a novice.

"I'm sure I'll manage." Mandie kept her tone light as she reached for the reins. She'd ridden horses since childhood, though always sidesaddle. Her skills might be a bit rusty, and she'd never ridden astride, but she could handle a horse.

She smiled and thanked him as he helped boost her into the saddle. Let him think her a beginner if it would make him speak to her.

She settled onto Rosie's back, and the mare shifted, finding her balance with the added weight. Mandie automatically tightened her thighs, but forced herself to relax. Riding astride felt odd at first, but the freedom of movement was wonderful.

As she settled into the saddle, Enoch mounted his own horse, a sturdy black gelding. He glanced over at her, seeming to check her seat and hand position. Apparently satisfied, he loosened his reins and started off at an easy walk.

They rode in silence for a while, the only sounds those of horse hooves clacking on stone and the creaking of leather.

She searched for something to say, some neutral topic to break the tension, but her mind went blank. All she could think about was the last time they'd been alone together...that kiss. The way Enoch's lips had felt on hers, the heat of his body pressed close.

She shook her head to dislodge the memory. It wouldn't do to dwell on such thoughts, not when Enoch seemed determined to forget the incident entirely.

Instead, she focused on the scenery around them. They climbed up a rocky slope, then over a pass between two mountain peaks. Birds wheeled overhead against the overcast sky, their cries echoing in the crisp morning air. She took a deep breath, filling her lungs with the scent of pine and fresh grass. This was exactly what she needed.

They rode on, the weather warming, though thick clouds hid the sun.

Enoch seemed content with the silence, his gaze scanning the horizon as if searching for something.

Mandie tried to relax into the easy rhythm of Rosie's gait, but a niggling worry wormed its way into her thoughts. What if Enoch regretted bringing her along? What if he found her mere presence a burden? Did he regret asking her to marry him?

Just as she opened her mouth to start a bit of conversation, Enoch reined in his horse on the downhill slope. "Storm's coming." His voice came low, almost a growl.

She followed his gaze to the western sky. Dark clouds had gathered, heavy and ominous. The air felt charged, the wind picking up with a chill. How had she not noticed?

He eyed her, maybe for the first time in over a day. "You want to turn back?"

She shook her head. "I'll be fine." She lifted her chin, trying to project more confidence than she felt. "We've come this far. Might as well finish the job."

Enoch's mouth tightened, but he nudged his horse forward. "Stay close then. If the weather gets worse, we'll find shelter."

As they rode, the wind whipped at her clothes and tugged strands of hair from her braid.

The first fat drops of rain splattered against her cheeks, cold and sharp.

Thunder rumbled in the distance, making Rosie snort and toss her head. Mandie tightened her grip on the reins and eased her legs so she didn't feed her tension to the horse.

The storm broke in full force as they crested the next rise. Sheets of rain lashed down, driven by gusts that threatened to unseat Mandie. Lightning streaked across the sky, followed by a crash of thunder that made both horses dance.

Enoch guided them off the trail and into a stand of pines that provided some shelter from the pounding rain.

"There's a cave not far ahead," he shouted over the roar of the storm. "We can wait it out there."

Mandie nodded. Her teeth had already begun to chatter from being soaked through in the biting wind.

They pushed on, and she bent low against the rain as Rosie picked her way over the slick, rocky trail.

Until they finally reached the dark mouth of a cave tucked into the mountainside.

Shelter, at last.

They dismounted at the cave entrance, and Enoch reached for her reins. "Get inside. I'll tie them and be there soon."

Mandie ducked into the cave, blinking as her eyes adjusted to the dimness. The space was larger than she'd expected, the ceiling high enough that Enoch should be able to stand without stooping. The air smelled of dank earth and something else musky and wild.

She moved farther in, away from the water streaming in rivulets from the entrance. The cave must have a slight downward slope toward the back.

She took up a space against the side wall, far away from the wind blowing in the entrance. Her shivers had worsened, and she wrapped her arms around herself. The fabric of her split skirt clung to her legs.

Enoch stepped inside a moment later, his broad shoulders outlined against the daylight outside. Water streamed from his hat and clothes, dripping onto the stone floor. He removed his hat and dropped it upside down onto a dry part of the floor. "Horses are as secure as they can be. I tied them under the overhang, so maybe they'll not get the worst of it." He joined her against the wall.

Mandie nodded, her teeth chattering too much for speech. She hugged herself tighter, trying to will warmth back into her limbs.

Enoch turned to look at her and frowned. "You're shaking."

"I'm f-fine." But a shiver slipped into her words, betraying her.

He looked around the space and down at himself. Neither of them had coats. Not in late summer. In Georgia, they wouldn't need a coat for two more months, even during a rain.

Enoch looked like he might strip off his shirt to give her, but thankfully, thought better of it. Instead he slipped a hand behind her back. "Come closer." He tugged her to him.

Maybe she should have resisted, especially the way he'd been acting yesterday and today. But she was so cold.

She snuggled into his chest. He wrapped those warm, strong arms around her, and his body heat seeped into her, chasing away the chill little by little. She sank into the steady rise and fall of his breathing, the thud of his heartbeat.

For a moment, the only sounds were the drumming of rain outside and the soft rustle of their clothing as he eased back against the rock wall behind him, bringing her along.

Mandie closed her eyes, savoring the closeness, the respite from the tension that had stretched between them.

Enoch's hand rubbed up and down her arm, almost absently, as if he'd forgotten he was doing it. The rough calluses on his palm and fingers tugged the damp fabric of her sleeve, sending a shiver through her that had nothing to do with the cold.

"I'm sorry," Enoch spoke abruptly, his voice a low rumble that she felt as much as heard. "For how I've acted lately."

Mandie tilted her head to look up at him. In the dim light, his face above his beard was all angles and shadows, his blue eyes nearly black. "What do you mean?"

He exhaled, his breath ruffling her hair. "I've been...distant. It's not fair to you."

She bit her lip, considering her words. "Is it…because of the kiss?"

Enoch tensed, his arm tightening around her. For a moment, she thought he wouldn't answer. Then, "Yes."

Her heart sank. "I'm sorry. I shouldn't have—"

"No." He cut her off, his voice rough. "Don't apologize. It's not your fault."

Mandie frowned. "Then why…?"

He was silent for so long, it didn't seem he would respond. "I don't know how to do this, Mandie."

Her insides tightened. "How to do—"

A sound broke through her words.

A low growl, somewhere back in the cave. Was that…?

Enoch stiffened, his hand going still on her arm. He eased his head toward the sound.

His grip on her tightened, and she turned to see what he'd seen.

At first, she could make out nothing in the darkness of the cave depths. Then two glowing eyes came clear.

They moved, and she caught the shadows of a head.

A cougar?

Her pulse thundered, her mind swimming for what to do. Would it attack? Did they have a weapon?

Enoch eased her sideways, moving out from between her and the wall. "When I say to, run for the entrance." His words came out barely more than a breath.

What was he going to do?

The animal padded forward a step, toward the daylight of the cave entrance, though it never seemed to take its eyes off them. She could see it better now, the grayish fur and the swinging tail.

Enoch shifted, reaching for his belt. The glint of a knife blade caught Mandie's eye.

He'd come armed, thank the Lord. But a knife against a

cougar? Even without the burns on his back, it wasn't a fair fight.

The animal crept a step toward them, muscles rippling beneath its sleek coat. Its ears flattened against its skull.

"Get ready." Enoch breathed the words, his body coiled tight as a spring.

Mandie's heart pounded against her ribs. She couldn't leave him to face this alone. Her gaze darted around, seeking anything she could use as a weapon. A rock, a stick, something.

The cougar snarled, a sound that raised every hair on Mandie's neck. It crouched, hindquarters bunching. Ready to spring.

"Now!" Enoch lunged forward just as the cat leapt, his knife slashing in a silvery arc.

Mandie bolted for the entrance, her boots slipping on the damp stone. Behind her, a yowl of pain echoed off the cave walls.

She had to help him.

CHAPTER 20

Mandie reached the mouth of the cave and whirled, searching frantically.

There. A fallen branch, just outside the opening, thick as her wrist. She snatched it up and spun back toward the fight.

Enoch and the cougar circled each other, the beast's eyes glinting with feral rage. Blood matted its fur where Enoch's knife had found its mark, and crimson stained the ripped sleeve on his forearm.

The animal lunged again, claws extended, and Enoch twisted away, slashing with his blade.

But the cougar's reflexes were lightning fast. It swiped with a massive paw, catching Enoch's shoulder and sending him staggering back.

Mandie didn't hesitate. With a cry, she charged forward, the branch raised high. She brought it down with all her strength across the cougar's hindquarters.

The animal yowled in pain and surprise, whirling to face this new threat.

Enoch seized the opening, driving his knife into its side. The cougar screeched and spun back to him.

Mandie swung again, catching it across the face. It reeled back, blood spattering the floor.

Enoch pressed the advantage, stabbing and slashing, driving the beast back. It swiped at him, but he dodged.

With a final, defiant snarl, the cougar turned and fled, disappearing into the rain.

Mandie stood frozen, chest heaving, the branch still raised.

Enoch sagged back against the cave wall, his knife clattering to the floor as he clutched at his left shoulder. Blood seeped through his fingers.

"Enoch!" She dropped the branch and rushed to him, her heart in her throat. She reached for his arm, trying to see how badly he was hurt. "Let me look."

He shook his head, jaw clenched tight. "It's not deep. Just a scratch."

She gave him a sharp glare. "It's more than a scratch. Please let me see."

Reluctantly, he eased his hand away. His sleeve hung in tatters, revealing four parallel gashes scoring his upper arm, oozing blood.

Enoch's chest still rose and fell as he fought to catch his breath. "I told you to run."

She was standing so close, the warmth of his words brushed her face, but she kept her focus on his injuries. "And leave you alone with that beast? Not likely." The bleeding seemed to already be slowing, but they needed to get him back to the house so she could clean up the entire arm.

She stepped back. "Think we can make it to the ranch?"

He glanced toward the cave opening. "I'd like to check on the cattle first. We're close to that pasture."

Frustration washed through her. "Enoch, you're really hurt. I'm sure one of your brothers would gladly come later to check the herd."

She laid a hand on his good arm and worked to soften her

voice so this next part didn't make him balk. "You take the brunt of every job on yourself. Let the rest of us help you for once."

Resistance flashed in his gaze, as she'd expected. What had made this man think he had to carry the weight of the world just to make the load lighter for everyone around him? Did he think he deserved to be punished for something? If only she could ask him.

But now, when they were both soaked through and blood dripped down his arm, wasn't the time. She settled for an added, "Please," and gave his good arm a little squeeze.

His gaze softened. "All right."

She could almost hear the, *Just this once,* he surely added in his mind. One battle at a time.

He reached down for his knife and stepped around her. "Let me go out first. Make sure he's not still out there."

She allowed him to lead, and as soon as he gave the *all-clear* sign, she followed him to the horses.

She started to offer Enoch help to mount, but he managed with little trouble. As though this was a daily experience, he climbed aboard his horse with his left arm clamped tight to his side.

She swung up onto Rosie's back, gathering the reins in hands that still trembled. The rain had slackened to a cold drizzle, but the wind cut through her damp clothes like a knife.

The journey back to the ranch felt like an eternity with the trail turned to a slick ribbon of mud by the rain. Rosie picked her way carefully, ears flicking back and forth at the rumble of thunder in the distance. Mandie's thighs ached from gripping the saddle, her split skirt plastered to her legs.

When they neared the house, Rosie loosed a whinny, which was answered by a horse in the barn. Willow probably, for she and her leggy filly were the only two in the structure these days.

Through the open barn doors, Robert poked his head out.

He strode out to meet them as they reined in by the front porch, and his eyes widened when he saw Enoch's arm.

"What happened?" Robert reached for Enoch's reins as he dismounted.

"Cougar in a cave." Enoch's voice was tight. "It's dealt with."

Robert's gaze flicked to Mandie, frowning at her bedraggled state and the blood on her hands from Enoch's wound. She must look a fright. "You two all right?"

Mandie nodded, sliding down from Rosie's back. Her legs nearly buckled, but she caught herself by gripping the saddle. "We will be. Enoch needs tending to."

"I'll see to the horses." Robert led them toward the barn. "You get him inside."

Mandie hurried to Enoch's side as he climbed the porch steps, ready to offer support if needed.

But he moved under his own power, though his jaw clenched beneath his beard. He didn't stop to remove his wet boots outside, which was good, for she would have insisted he leave them on. She could wipe up a little muddy water later.

Once he reached the kitchen, he shrugged out of his ruined shirt, revealing the angry red gashes on his shoulder and upper arm, a painful addition to the barely healed burns.

Stripped to the waist, the damage looked even worse. The slashes still seeped blood. Bruises were already forming, dark splotches that made her body ache in sympathy.

"Sit." Mandie pointed to a chair, her tone brooking no argument. "I'll get hot water and bandages."

He obeyed without protest and sank onto the wooden seat. Exhaustion and pain lined his face, making him look older than his years.

She hurried to grab two bowls, filling one with water from the ever-present kettle on the stove, and then pulled the crate of bandaging supplies down from the shelf. Had it only been four days since she'd been here, doing nearly this exact thing?

He sat without a shirt, same as last time, though now he'd not bothered with a blanket over his good shoulder. The burns were indeed healing, but now they also had to make sure these claw marks didn't fester.

His head slumped in his right hand, revealing the thickness of the ropy muscles across his shoulders and the top of his back.

She set the bowls and crate on the table, then moved to his side and gripped his palm to stretch his arm out so she could get a good look at all the lacerations.

The gashes were raw and jagged, still bleeding a little. Mandie moved an empty basin under his arm, then dipped a clean cloth in the warm water and squeezed liquid over the first cut. Enoch flinched but held still, his muscles taut under her fingers.

One by one, she did the same for each claw mark, pausing over one near the middle.

"This is going to need sewing up." She lifted her focus to meet his gaze. In the light of the kitchen, his eyes were the color of a stormy sea. "I can do it, if you'll let me."

Something flickered in his expression, there and gone too fast for her to read. "Do it." He bobbed his chin toward the crate. "Pour whiskey on them first. Cougar scratches fester easy."

She glanced at the small amber bottle tucked under the bandages. That would sting nearly as bad as the stitches.

Keeping the basin under his arm, she splashed a liberal amount of the liquid over the gashes.

Enoch hissed through his teeth at the first touch but held himself still as she worked. She could feel the tension thrumming through him, the barely leashed power in his muscles. Like a wild thing, only half-tamed.

As she cleaned the wounds, she studied the scars marking his skin farther down his arm—old wounds, long healed. What other hurts had he endured in his life? Had these affected his body only? Or his heart too?

When the wounds were clean, she threaded a needle, her hands surprisingly steady despite the tumult of emotions swirling inside her. She'd never stitched a person before, only fabric. But the principle was the same, wasn't it? In and out, neat and even.

She took a deep breath and bent over his arm, the needle poised. "Ready?"

"Get on with it." The words were a low growl.

The first pierce of the needle made him flinch, a barely perceptible tightening of his jaw. But he held himself still as she worked, stitching the wound closed with tiny movements. Blood welled up, staining her fingers, but she dabbed it away and kept going.

In and out, a steady rhythm, until the gash was sealed with a line of neat stitches.

She tied off the thread and snipped the excess, then applied salve and reached for the bandages. As she wound the strips of cotton around his arm, her fingertips brushed the inside of his arm, feeling the heat of him, the thrum of his pulse.

Enoch watched her work, his gaze heavy on her bent head. She could feel the weight of it, the unspoken questions hanging in the air between them.

When the last bandage was secured, she straightened, meeting his eyes. "There. That should hold."

"Thank you." His voice was a low rumble, like distant thunder.

Mandie nodded. They were so close. She couldn't help but watch from the corner of her eye as his bare chest rose and fell with each breath. Did she dare ask him what he'd been about to say in the cave?

She could still feel his arms around her as he'd held her close, the raw vulnerability in his voice when he'd said he didn't know how to do this. Whatever *this* was.

She sank into the chair around the corner from his and

placed her hands on the table to draw his focus to her. Before she could lose her courage, she spoke. "What did you mean in the cave when you said you didn't know how to do this?"

Enoch's gaze dropped to her hands on the table, then lifted back to her face. In the soft light from the window, the planes and angles of his features seemed even more chiseled, as if carved from stone. But there was a vulnerability in his eyes, a rawness that made her heart ache.

He exhaled, a long breath. "I don't know how to let someone in, Mandie. How to...care for someone, and still prepare to lose them."

Mandie's throat tightened. She could hear the old pain in his voice, the wounds that went soul-deep. "You've lost someone before."

Enoch's jaw clenched, a muscle ticking near his eye. "My mother, when I was a boy. And my father, in a way, when he left us here and went back to England."

Her chest squeezed. She wanted to reach out and place her hand on his, to offer comfort. But something in his expression made it seem like there was more.

His gaze turned distant, focused on some point beyond her. His throat worked, like he was fighting with himself over whether to say the rest. When he spoke, a rasp roughened his voice. "I was to be married once, but she was taken too. Her entire family, in a wagon accident." His eyes hardened as he flicked them back to her. "Mrs. Wang's husband when his heart gave out. And most recently, my older brother, leaving me to take on a life I never wanted."

His tone had lost all softness by the end, and his eyes flashed. "It took me a while to learn not to get too attached. But I've finally taken the lesson well."

Her heart cracked at the pain in his words, the raw anguish beneath his hard gaze. How could one man bear so much loss, so much sorrow, and still stand tall? Still find the strength to care for his family, his land, even if he tried to hold himself apart?

She reached across the table, slowly, giving him time to pull away. When he didn't, she laid her hand over his, feeling the roughness of his knuckles, the strength in his fingers. "I'm so sorry, Enoch. I can't imagine the hurt you've endured."

He stared at their joined hands, his jaw working. "It's in the past. I've learned to live with it."

"But you haven't learned to live beyond it." She gentled her tone, willing him to hear her. "You've closed yourself off, thinking it will protect you. But all it's doing is keeping you from the thing you need most."

His gaze flicked up to hers, wary. "And what's that?"

"Love." The word hung between them, soft but unyielding. "Connection. The knowledge that you're not alone, even in your pain."

Enoch's hand tensed under hers, but he didn't pull away. "I have my family. My brothers."

"And they love you. Fiercely. But you hold even them at a distance. Always the strong one, the caretaker, never letting them see your own hurts and needs." Mandie swallowed. "You don't have to be strong all the time, Enoch. You're allowed to lean on others. To let them help carry your burdens."

He looked away, his profile stark against the light from the window. "I'm not sure I know how."

She squeezed his hand. "You start by trusting. By taking small steps, one at a time. Like you did today, letting me come with you, even though it scared you."

His gaze swung back to hers, surprise flicking in those blue depths. "I wasn't…"

A small smile tugged at her lips. "I could see it in your eyes. The hesitation, the way you nearly said no. But you took a chance, even if it was just to stop my pestering." She let the grin out a little. "And look what happened. We faced down a cougar together. We made a pretty good team, don't you think?"

Something softened in his expression. "We did. You... surprised me out there. The way you charged back swinging that branch."

She huffed a laugh. "I couldn't leave you to face that beast alone. I had to do something."

"You might well have saved my life." Enoch's voice came low. His hand turned under hers, his fingers curling around her palm. "Thank you, Mandie. Truly."

Her heart swelled at his words, at the rare openness in his gaze. She loved this side he so rarely showed—the man beneath the stoic exterior, the one who felt deeply and cared fiercely, even if he tried to hide it.

She wanted to see more of that man. To know him, in all his strengths and vulnerabilities.

But it would take time. Patience.

He'd built his walls high and thick, and it would take more than one conversation, one near-death experience, to breach them fully.

For now, this was enough. This small step forward, this moment of connection.

She smiled at him, letting her fingers twine with his. "You're welcome. I'm just glad we both made it back in one piece."

"More or less." Enoch glanced at his bandaged arm with a wry twist of his lips.

Mandie chuckled. "Nothing a little time and care won't mend."

She could only pray the same could be said for his heart. Given time, care, and God's grace, surely even the deepest hurts could heal.

She gave his hand a final squeeze, then pulled back. As much as she wanted to linger in this moment, she had work she should attend to.

She stood, smoothing her damp, muddy skirt. "I should change out of these wet things."

Enoch nodded, his gaze following her as she rose. "I should do the same." He glanced down at his bare chest, and he seemed to come back to himself.

He pushed to his feet and followed her out of the kitchen, then down the hall toward their separate rooms.

* * *

THE FIRE POPPED in the hearth as Enoch stared into the flames, his bandaged arm stiff at his side. The house had finally quieted, and he was fairly certain Mandie lay asleep in her chamber.

But his body still couldn't rest.

Footsteps sounded from the kitchen, and James ambled into the room, a piece of cornbread in his hand. His younger brother sank into the chair opposite him, then studied him as he chewed. That glint in his eye made Enoch's neck itch.

At last, James swallowed and spoke. "I heard you and Mandie in the kitchen. Sounds like the two of you are getting along."

Enoch tightened his jaw. He didn't want to say it, but the words came anyway. "I almost lost her today."

James stayed quiet a moment as he chewed. But then he swallowed, and his tone came out matter-of-fact. "She's safe. You chased the cat off."

"This time." Enoch snapped the words, then forced his tone to soften. "But what if I can't next time? What if—" He stopped. He didn't need to say the words for his brother to know his meaning.

James leaned forward. "You're falling for her, aren't you?" Enoch wasn't about to answer that, but of course James pressed on. "And it terrifies you because you've lost too much already."

Enoch's hands balled into fists. "I can't do it again, James.

Losing Charlotte...it broke me. And then Will. If I let her in and she's taken too..."

James raised his brows. "You think keeping her at arm's length will hurt less? You're already past that point."

He clenched his fists tighter. He wanted to haul back and slug his brother. James might be right, but he didn't have to be so smug about it.

But Enoch forced himself to keep still.

He *was* past the point of falling for her. Every glance, every touch from Mandie pulled him deeper.

Today, when she'd faced the cougar with him, he'd known it —he'd fight anything to keep her safe. "I don't know how to love her and not be afraid," he admitted, voice rough.

James nodded. "Maybe you don't have to. Maybe the fear's part of it. But she's worth it, Enoch. You know that."

Enoch swallowed hard. He wasn't sure he could face that truth. Not yet. Maybe not ever.

CHAPTER 21

Enoch swung the barn doors wide, meeting Willow's nicker of greeting. He paused to scratch the mare's neck and let the filly sniff his hand. It had been nearly three weeks since the barn had burned. This morning he'd peered into the glass, happy to see that the ugly burn creeping up his neck and into his hair had mellowed into pink new skin. Even better, he could move his left shoulder without the constant twinge of a deep scab. Now only the deepest of the cat scratches still tugged as he turned to the wagon tucked in the corner on the other side of the aisle.

Today they could finally pick up the lumber from Walnut Springs to finish the barn.

He strode to the wagon and checked the wheels, running a hand along the spokes to test for any wobble or weakness. All seemed in good repair.

He couldn't let anything go wrong today, not with Mandie riding along to town with him and James.

Two days had passed since that wet ride and cougar attack, and he'd had a feeling she would jump at another chance to get out of the house. She had.

He could understand her restlessness. Being cooped up inside, even a house as large as this one, could make a body feel trapped after a while. Especially someone used to the freedoms of being on her own.

Still, a part of him wished she would stay safely at the ranch, away from any dangers or discomforts the journey might bring. It would be a long, bumpy ride in her condition, and he didn't want to risk her health or the babe's.

But the hopeful look on her face had weakened his resolve. After their conversation in the kitchen, he found it harder to deny her, to keep that careful distance between them. So against his better judgment, he'd agreed. And maybe…maybe by coming to town, she'd remember how nice and convenient everything was and want to stay. She'd be safer here than on the ranch, where wildcats and barn fires sprang up without warning. Safer here than with *him*.

When he'd agreed to let her come, her smile had been radiant, making something in his chest tighten. *Thank you, Enoch. I promise I won't be any trouble.*

Mandie Beaumont was trouble incarnate, at least for his peace of mind.

He couldn't seem to stop thinking about her, worrying about her, wanting to be near her, despite all his best efforts to maintain his walls.

Thankfully, James strode into the barn just in time to distract him. That ever-present grin marked his face. "You ready for our adventure?"

Enoch straightened, dusting off his hands. "Not an adventure. Just a supply run." But he couldn't quite keep the edge of tension from his voice.

James cocked an eyebrow. "With Mandie along? I'd say that qualifies as an adventure." His grin turned sly. "Especially given the way you two have been dancing around each other lately."

Enoch shot him a sharp look. "I don't know what you're talking about."

"Sure you don't." James chuckled and moved to grab the harnesses. "Just try not to scowl at her the whole way. Poor woman might think you don't like her company."

Enoch bit back a retort. He liked Mandie's company far too much. That was the problem.

And he didn't want to hurt her by keeping her out. Perhaps she'd be happier somewhere else. She'd mentioned she had money. Maybe while they were in town, he could find a way to set her up safely somewhere. Maybe Two Stones would help.

The two of them made quick work of hitching the team, as well as saddling the mount James would ride. The wagon bench could hold three if they squeezed together, but on the return trip, the horses would have the weight of all the lumber. Besides, the last thing he needed was Mandie's body pressed up against his side all the way to town and back. Or James's side, for that matter.

By the time they led the horses out into the yard, the morning sun had crested the mountains, painting the sky in shades of gold and pink.

Mandie must have been watching for them, for she stepped from the house as Enoch reined in the team by the porch steps.

She wore a pale blue dress, her dark hair braided and coiled at the nape of her neck. When her eyes met his, a small smile curved her lips, equal parts shy and excited.

Enoch's heart gave a traitorous thump.

Her gaze shifted to take in his brother too. "Good morning."

James swept off his hat and dipped a gallant bow from his saddle. "And a fine morning it is, now that you've graced us with your presence."

Mandie laughed, a warm, rich sound that filled the air. "Ever the charmer, James. I see the trip ahead has done nothing to dull your wit."

"Wit?" James placed a hand over his heart. "You wound me, Mandie. I assure you, my compliments spring from the deepest sincerity."

She shook her head, still smiling. "Sincere or not, I thank you for them. It's a lovely start to the day."

Enoch cleared his throat. "We should get moving if we want to make good time." He dismounted from the wagon as she descended the porch.

He took the carpetbag from her and placed it to the side so he could use both hands to lift her to the bench. He wasn't prepared for her softness. Her warmth. The feel of her curves beneath his palms.

When she slid onto the seat, pulling out of his reach, he had to force himself to focus on something other than reaching for her again.

Mandie smoothed her skirts and flashed him a smile. "Thank you."

He gave a curt nod and grabbed her bag, stowing it under the bench before climbing up beside her. The wagon dipped and creaked under his weight. He was a clumsy ox compared to her fluid grace.

James nudged his horse alongside them. "Ready?"

Enoch nodded, then flicked the reins for the team to follow in behind his brother's mount.

As the wagon rolled down the dirt track, he couldn't help but be aware of Mandie's presence beside him. The sway and jolt of the wagon bench brought them into contact more than once, her shoulder and thigh brushing his.

He kept his gaze fixed ahead, trying to ignore the scent of her hair, the soft rhythm of her breaths. But it was a losing battle. His senses felt heightened, attuned to her every movement.

Mandie seemed oblivious to his inner turmoil, her face alight with quiet happiness as she took in the passing scenery.

"It's so beautiful out here. I don't think I could ever tire of these mountains."

Enoch darted a glance at her, taking in the soft smile on her lips, the way the sunlight brought out glints of red in her dark hair. She looked radiant, alive in a way he rarely saw within the confines of the house. "You like being outdoors."

She turned to him, her eyes bright. "I do. I always have, even as a child. There's something freeing about open spaces, about being surrounded by nature's beauty." Her smile turned wistful. "In Savannah, I often felt...confined. By the expectations of society, the strict rules of propriety. Out here, it's different. Simpler, in a way, but also more real. Here, I feel like I can breathe. Like I can just be myself, without all the trappings and expectations."

This woman. She'd so completely echoed what pressed inside his own chest. She'd put into words what he felt each time he rode out into the mountains, looked over the peaks and valleys that stretched farther than any city street could hope to.

Out here, all the duties and restrictions that came with his family title faded away, leaving only him. The man who craved simplicity, who felt most at home under an open sky, with the scent of pine and damp earth in his lungs.

As he glanced down at her upturned face, something shifted inside him.

He swallowed, searching for a response that wouldn't reveal too much. "I know what you mean. The mountains, the land...they have a way of stripping away all the unnecessary things. Leaving only what's true and essential."

Her smile deepened, warming him like a touch. "Yes. Exactly."

She held his gaze, and for a heartbeat, a connection sparked between them, an understanding that went beyond words.

Then James called back to them, pointing out a hawk circling overhead, and the moment passed.

But as they rode on, occasionally speaking of inconsequential things, he couldn't get that brief exchange out of his mind.

Maybe he and Mandie had more in common than he'd ever guessed.

That thought made him want to draw closer to her, even as instinct screamed for him to pull back. To protect himself.

Yet he was so tired of being alone. Of holding himself apart, aloof and untouchable. With Mandie, he couldn't stop longing for...more. Even if he didn't quite know what that meant. Or whether reaching for it was safe.

The miles fell away beneath the wagon wheels, the sun climbing higher into the cloudless blue sky. Before long, Walnut Springs stretched out in the valley before them. As they neared the main road through town, the sounds of men's shouts and pounding hammers rose from the sawmill by the river. When Clark had an order to fill, that cacophony usually overshadowed all the other noises from the town.

Walnut Springs wasn't large, but it held a mercantile with the telegraph office inside. And of course the doctor. A scattering of other businesses lined the street—a blacksmith, a cafeteria with a few rooms upstairs they let out to travelers, a washwoman, and the like. But the mercantile and sawmill were the two businesses the Balfours frequented the most.

Holbrook at the mercantile could order most anything they needed if they were willing to wait long enough—and pay the stout shipping fees.

Enoch reined in the team in front of the sawmill, then set the brake and jumped to the ground. He sent a glance to his brother before reaching to help Mandie down. "You want to see Clark and back the wagon in so they can start loading? I'll take Mandie to the mercantile, and you can meet us there."

Mandie placed her hand in his as she reached her boot down to the step. Her hands were so soft, he almost felt guilty letting her touch his callused fingers. But he also wasn't above enjoying her touch.

When she settled on the ground, she sent him a warm smile. "Thank you."

James cleared his throat, forcing Enoch to look away from that ray of sunshine to his brother's frowning face. "How about you talk to Clark, and I'll take Mandie to the mercantile? You're the one who drove the wagon here. Finish the job."

Enoch wanted to growl. Maybe even snap at his brother like a stray mongrel.

But James had a point. Any argument he came back with would sound petty and entitled.

So he only nodded, but the glare he sent the back of his brother's head as the cad extended his arm to Mandie should have been hot enough to set fire to that brown fluff James had clearly taken extra care to pomade in place today.

As the pair walked away, James's mount trailing behind, Enoch turned back to the sawmill and sighed. It seemed duty over pleasure would never end for him.

CHAPTER 22

The wagon creaked and groaned, straining under the weight of the lumber as it rolled up the rocky trail. Mandie leaned back against the bench, her mind still spinning with the memories of their refreshing day in town.

Having the chance to shop again had turned out to be far more refreshing than she'd expected. The Walnut Grove Mercantile possessed a surprising variety of goods, and they'd enjoyed a pleasant lunch at the little cafeteria that served as the lower level to the boarding house.

James had been attentive and charming as always, his quick wit and easy laughter drawing her out of her shell.

And Enoch... Well, he'd been Enoch. Gruff and taciturn at first, clearly irked by his brother's flirtations. But as the day wore on, he appeared to relax, his stern facade softening around the edges.

It had been nice to feel like a normal woman for once. Not a grieving widow or an invalid. Simply a lady enjoying the company of two handsome gentlemen.

Even if one of those gentlemen was simply being a pleasant younger brother, and the other...

The other stirred feelings in her that were far from sisterly.

She darted a glance at Enoch, taking in his strong profile, the way his hands gripped the reins with quiet competence. He'd removed his hat, and the breeze ruffled his dark hair, revealing the twisted scar he'd received saving Willow and her baby. Did it still hurt? The thought made her fingers itch to smooth his locks back from his brow.

Dragging her gaze away, she focused on the passing scenery. The heavy load of wood in the bed made the wagon creak and groan more than before, nearly drowning out the birdsong and rustle of leaves on the trail. They were lumbering around the side of the mountain, but the road was wide enough that the rig stayed away from the downward slope on her side. It wasn't a cliff exactly, just a steep hill.

The front wheel on Enoch's side hit a particularly deep rut, lurching the wagon forward. She fought to hold in a gasp as she clutched the seat for balance.

Enoch's arm shot out in front of her, a brace to keep her in place even as he gripped both reins tighter in his other hand, holding the team steady when the rear wheel dropped into the rut too. "You all right?"

She managed a nod. "I'm fine. Just startled."

When the rig settled again, he glanced her way. His gaze searched her face, as though looking for details of an injury she'd not confessed to. He must be satisfied, for he turned forward again. "The road's a bit rough through here. We'll take it slow."

True to his word, he eased the horses into a slower pace, guiding the wagon around rocks and over uneven patches of ground.

She tried to relax, but every bump and sway seemed magnified, jangling her nerves a little tighter each time.

They navigated a narrow stretch, though the incline leveled out some through the length of it.

As they rounded the next bend, the trail widened once more. Mandie let out a breath. But just as she started to relax, the wagon hit another deep rut, larger than any of the previous ones.

The wagon lurched violently to the side. Wood planks clattered and shifted behind them. Enoch barked a command to the horses, hauling back on the reins to steady the team even as the rig tipped precariously toward the slope.

Mandie's stomach swooped. She grabbed for the seat, for Enoch, for anything solid as her world tilted. But gravity yanked her sideways.

Her hip struck the edge of the bench. Then she was falling, tumbling over the side of the wagon into open air.

Brush and saplings broke her fall, but she still hit the ground with a jarring thud. All the breath left her lungs.

She rolled, leaves and twigs catching in her hair, snagging her skirts. Down and down, until she fetched up against the base of a tree, her back pressed against the bark.

For a moment, she could only lie there, stunned and gasping. Pain throbbed through her, radiating from her side, her hip, her head.

But worse than that was the sharp stab low in her belly, like a knife twisting.

No. Oh God, no!

Panic clawed up her throat. She curled inward, hands clutching her stomach. "Please." Her jaw trembled as she whispered the words. "Please be all right."

Dimly, she heard Enoch shouting her name, the crashing of footsteps down the hill.

He dropped to his knees beside her, fear etched all over his face. "Mandie! Are you hurt?" His hands hovered over her, as if afraid to touch.

She tried to speak, but a whimper escaped instead. Tears blurred her vision. "The baby."

Enoch paled.

Carefully, so carefully, he gathered her into his arms. "I've got you." His voice rasped thick with emotion. "Just hold on."

He carried her up the embankment, cradling her against his chest. Each step sent a fresh wave of pain through her, but she clung to him, her face pressed into the solid column of his neck.

Tears stung, but she blinked them back. She had to be strong now. For the baby. For Enoch.

At the top, he lowered her onto the wagon bench. "James," he barked. "Secure the load. We need to get her home. Now."

James replied to him, but he spoke quietly, and the chaos inside her drowned out his words. She focused on breathing, slow and steady. The pain in her belly had subsided, and she strained for any sensation that might be the baby moving around. It had only happened a few times since that first day when she'd realized she carried a child, so not feeling movement now wouldn't be unusual.

But surely after such a harrowing tumble, her wee one would have a reaction.

Enoch appeared beside her, his face close enough that she could see the murky shadows clouding his eyes. "One of the axles snapped. I'm going to take you on the gelding."

She pushed up to her elbow so she could better figure out what he was saying.

Before she could respond, he slid his arm beneath her shoulders, the other under her knees, and then he was lifting her, pulling her tight against his chest. She gasped at the movement, her hands clutching at his shirt.

"I can walk." The protest came out weak, even as she pressed her face into his shoulder.

"I'm not taking any chances." His low voice vibrated through her.

He carried her to where James stood with his horse. "Can

you stand for a minute? Until I'm in the saddle?" His words rumbled near her ear, his breath fanning her nose.

She nodded, and he eased her feet to the ground, keeping a firm arm around her waist as she swayed. Her legs felt like jelly, the ground unsteady beneath her, but his solid presence kept her upright.

James gripped her arm as Enoch pulled away. Being so fully cared for by these men…it eased the knot in her chest at least a little.

A moment later, Enoch had settled into the saddle, and she started to lift her foot to the stirrup. Was she to sit behind him? She didn't have on her split skirt.

But James lifted her waist, and Enoch reached for her upper arms. "Turn and sit across my lap."

She tried to obey, though the movement was awkward. She plopped down onto his lap harder than she'd intended, drawing a grunt from him.

Heat flooded up her neck. "Sorry." She tried to shift her weight to find a more ladylike pose, but pain shot through her hip, and she gasped.

Enoch's arm tightened around her waist. "Easy." His other hand cupped the back of her head, guiding it to rest on his shoulder. "Just lean on me. I've got you."

Too weary and sore to argue, she let her body melt into his, her face nestling into the warm crook of his neck, her arms loose around his waist. The steady thrum of his pulse beat against her cheek, and she focused on that, on the rise and fall of his chest as he breathed.

He smelled of leather and pine and sweat and something uniquely Enoch. Solid. Safe.

CHAPTER 23

Enoch's knuckles whitened on the reins as the ranch house came into view, his heart pounding a desperate rhythm against his ribs. He drew the gelding to a stop and slid to the ground, keeping Mandie in his arms.

She clung to him, her face pale and pinched, and the sight sliced through him like a blade.

"I've got you." He cradled her close as he strode toward the house. "You're going to be fine. Both of you."

But even as the words left his lips, a sickening sense of familiarity swept over him. A wagon accident. It was Charlotte all over again.

No. He wouldn't let that happen again. Couldn't bear it.

He shouldered open the door and carried Mandie straight to her room, easing her onto her quilt.

She whimpered as he pulled his arms from beneath her, and the sound cleaved his heart in two.

"I'll send Robert for the doctor." He smoothed a hand over her hair, his touch lingering a moment longer than necessary. "Thomas can help James with the wagon. You just rest now."

Her fingers caught his sleeve as he started to pull away.

"Enoch, I..." She swallowed hard, her eyes luminous with unshed tears. "Thank you. For saving me and getting me home safe."

Something in his chest constricted, and a fist of emotion lodged behind his breastbone. He wanted to gather her close, to hold her until the fear and pain drained away. But he couldn't afford to let himself feel that deeply. Not again.

He should have found a safer place for her, but he hadn't been able to follow through with the idea. Had selfishly kept her for himself. He was a cad.

Carefully, he untangled her fingers from his sleeve. "Rest now. I'll be back to check on you soon." His voice emerged rougher than he intended, scraped raw by the terror still clawing at his insides.

He slipped out of the room before she could reply, closing the door with a soft click. For a long moment, he simply leaned against the solid wood, his eyes squeezing shut as he drew a shuddering breath.

Dear God, please let them be all right. He couldn't lose Mandie and the baby. Not like he'd lost Charlotte. Her family. Will. So many people.

The old grief, never far from the surface, surged up his throat, hot and bitter. He shoved it down with force of will.

He couldn't afford to wallow in the past. Mandie needed him here, now, in the present. Later he'd figure out what to do with their future.

Straightening, he strode out to the porch where Robert and Thomas were carrying saddles from the pasture. "Robert, ride for the doctor." Enoch's voice came out harsher than he intended. "There was a wagon accident, and Mandie took a bad fall. I brought her back to the house and she's resting now."

His middle brother's eyes widened, but he nodded and spun to saddle a horse.

Enoch turned to Thomas. "Go help James fix the axle. It

snapped in that narrow stretch on Turner's slope. I'll be inside with Mandie if you need anything."

Thomas tipped his hat. "We'll handle things. You just take care of her."

Enoch's throat tightened. He managed a curt nod before striding back to the house.

Inside, he tiptoed to Mandie's door and listened, just to see if it sounded like she needed anything. No noises drifted from inside, so he turned the knob and cracked it open. He shouldn't ignore her privacy like this, but he had to know she wasn't writhing in pain.

She lay where he'd left her, curled on her side atop the quilt. Her eyes were closed, the rise and fall of her shoulder slow and even. But was that a furrow between her brows? If so, from pain or worry?

He eased the door shut and retreated to the main room. He should try to work. Or maybe prepare food for when Mandie awoke.

But he could only sink into a chair by the cold fireplace. He let his head fall into his hands, the scars pulling on his skin, his heart.

The sickening lurch of fear rushed in, giving rise to overwhelming helplessness. Could he survive the agonizing wait to know if his world had shattered once more?

Why had he let Mandie ride in the wagon with a load that heavy? He should have insisted she stay safely at home, or at the very least, ride her own horse. With the risks of that heavy lumber, he never should have allowed her to be in harm's way.

He had failed both the women in his care. Failed to keep them safe. What kind of man was he, that he couldn't protect the ones he loved?

He sat there until he couldn't bear the oppressive weight of silence any longer. He needed fresh air, maybe an ax and logs to chop. Something to work out this turmoil inside him.

But he didn't dare leave Mandie. She could call for him at any moment. And he wouldn't desert her when she needed him.

Not enough time had passed when he heard the click of her bed chamber door open. His scrambled mind strained to make sense of why she would be up.

The soft padding of her slippers finally pulled him to his senses, and he spun, striding to meet her.

She stood at the end of the hallway, one hand braced against the wall, the other pressed to her belly. She'd refastened her hair, but her face was still pale. "I thought I would start food for the evening meal."

He reached her in two more strides and stopped where he could block her path to the kitchen. "Absolutely not. You need to be resting."

She raised a brow at him. "I feel much better. And you've been so busy worrying over me, I'm sure you haven't eaten."

His jaw clenched. "I'm fine. It's you I'm concerned about. I'll make food for you." He searched her face for any sign of lingering pain or distress. "Please, Mandie. Go back to bed. For my peace of mind, if nothing else."

Her expression softened. "I'm all right, Enoch. Truly. I just… I couldn't lie there any longer." She took a step to go around him.

He shifted to block her again, frustration welling in his throat. "Please, Mandie. I can't have you up doing more damage. What if…?" He couldn't bring himself to speak the thought aloud.

She reached out and touched his arm, and the contact made him pause. He forced in a breath. Willed his insides to settle enough to meet her gaze.

Those dark eyes were gentle as they searched his face. "How about if I rest on the sofa out here? That way I won't be locked away in the bed chamber."

He might have to live with that compromise. With a sigh, he nodded.

She smiled at him, a tired but genuine softening of her eyes. "Thank you."

He took her elbow and guided her to the sofa. She sank onto the cushions, arranging her skirts around her.

He stood awkwardly for a moment, like an empty-headed ox. "I'll get you a blanket." He needed something to occupy his hands, his mind. He strode to the chest by the fireplace and pulled out a soft woolen throw, carrying it back to tuck around her legs.

As he leaned over her, she caught his hand. "Enoch. I'm fine, truly. You don't need to fuss."

The warmth of her fingers seeped into his skin, and he had to resist the urge to turn his palm, to lace their fingers together.

He pulled away and straightened. "I'll make tea. And buttered cornbread, if you think you could eat."

She nodded. "That would be lovely, thank you."

He escaped to the kitchen. At least he could do something. The familiar motions of filling the kettle, slicing cornbread, gave him something to focus on besides the fear still churning in his gut.

By the time the tea had steeped and the bread was buttered, he'd managed to compose himself. He carried the tray out to her, setting it on the low table by the sofa.

She smiled up at him as she reached for the mug, her fingers brushing his. "Thank you, Enoch. This is perfect."

He nodded, unable to form words past the constriction in his throat. He sank into the armchair across from her, watching as she sipped the tea and nibbled at the cornbread.

The silence stretched between them, too thick.

Finally, Mandie set down her cup and met his gaze. "I felt the baby move. While I was resting."

His heart stuttered. "You did?"

She nodded, her hand drifting to her middle. "Just a flutter, but it was there. I think...I think everything is all right."

Relief crashed over him like a wave, so strong it left him lightheaded. He closed his eyes for a moment. *Thank You, God.*

When he opened them again, Mandie was watching him, her expression gentle.

He swallowed hard. "That's...good. I'm glad."

Her smile widened a fraction. "I thought maybe, while we wait for the doctor...you could teach me to play chess? I've always wanted to learn."

He stared at her, uncomprehending. How could she think of games at a time like this? When she'd nearly...when they'd almost...

But her eyes were earnest, hopeful. Clinging to normalcy in the midst of upheaval. He couldn't deny her. "I'll get the board."

He fetched the chessboard from its shelf and arranged the pieces, his hands needing the simple task to keep from shaking. As he explained the basic rules and moved the pieces to demonstrate, Mandie leaned forward, her brow furrowed in concentration.

The intellectual challenge seemed to bring color back to her cheeks, and the distraction helped him too, though part of him remained coiled tight with worry.

They played in near silence, the clack of pieces against the board the only sound besides the ticking of the mantel clock. She picked up the strategy quickly, her moves growing bolder and more calculated with each turn. Enoch had to focus to stay a step ahead of her.

Darkness had nearly settled by the time hoofbeats sounded outside.

He leapt to his feet, his heart pounding as he strode to the entryway and pulled open the door.

Robert swung down from his saddle, the doctor right behind him.

Enoch stepped aside to let them in, his pulse thundering in his ears. "She's resting on the sofa."

The doctor nodded, moving past him into the house with brisk efficiency. "I'll need to examine her privately."

Inside, Mandie had already stood. "Doctor Hansen. Thank you for coming."

The older man smiled. "Of course, my dear. Now, let's have a look at you, shall we?"

Robert clapped a hand on Enoch's shoulder as the two disappeared down the hallway. "She'll be all right, Enoch. You got her back safe."

Enoch shrugged off the touch, pacing to the window. He stared out at the darkening landscape without really seeing it, his mind a chaotic whirl.

Mandie's soft voice drifted from the other room, answered by the doctor's lower rumble.

Enoch strained to make out the words, but couldn't discern anything intelligible.

The minutes crawled by, each one an eternity. Robert went outside to tend to the stock, and Enoch moved back to pacing the length of the room. Would the doctor come out and say she'd lost the baby? *God, don't let her lose the baby.*

After what felt like hours, the doctor's boots sounded in the hallway. Enoch spun to face it, his heart in his throat.

The doctor emerged first, his expression unreadable. Mandie followed a step behind, and the moment Enoch saw her face, the coiled tension in his chest eased.

She was smiling. Tired and pale, but smiling.

The doctor turned to him. "Mrs. Beaumont and the baby both appear to be in good health. No signs of lasting injury from the fall."

Relief crashed through Enoch, so intense it left him lightheaded. He braced a hand against the wall so his knees didn't give way. "Thank God."

Mandie moved to his side, her hand resting on his arm. "I told you we were all right." Her voice was gentle, but held a note of admonishment.

He turned to her, drinking in the sight of her whole and well. The urge to pull her into his arms, to hold her close and never let go, surged through him. But he tamped it down, his jaw clenching with the effort. "You should rest." His voice came out nearly a growl.

Her smile faltered a fraction, but she nodded. "I will. But Enoch, please don't worry so."

While fear still clawed at his insides, sharp and relentless, he managed a tight nod. "I'll see the doctor out."

Enoch turned to the man. "Thank you for coming. For checking on her." He managed to keep his voice level, but inside, his emotions churned like storm-tossed waves.

The older man clapped him on the shoulder. "She'll be just fine, son. A few days of rest and she'll be good as new."

Enoch walked with the doctor outside, then as the man rode back toward town, Enoch stood for a long moment on the porch, drawing deep breaths of the cool evening air. The sky had darkened to indigo, the first stars winking into view.

Maybe time in the barn could ease the tangles inside him. He descended the porch steps and started toward the structure. Its burned shell stood out as a dark, awkward shadow. The charred remains mocked him, a physical form of his failures and losses.

He clenched his fists, his nails biting into his palms. He shouldn't be so angry. The doctor had said she was *fine*. She and the baby both.

He was halfway across the yard when the sound of an approaching wagon made him pause. He turned to see James and Thomas in the damaged rig.

James reined the team to a stop in front of the barn and swung down from the seat. "How is she?"

Enoch swallowed past the tightness in his throat. "The

doctor says she'll be fine." The words tasted bitter on his tongue, as if saying them aloud might somehow alter their truth.

Relief softened his brother's features. "Thank God. We can put the team up if you want to go back inside to her."

Enoch shook his head. "I'll unharness them. You two go in and scrounge up some food. I'm sure you're hungry and tired."

James studied him. Then he spoke in a lower voice. "Go on in, Thomas. Enoch and I can handle this."

Their baby brother nodded and trudged toward the house, leaving Enoch and James alone in the deepening night.

James was the next brother in line after him, and he'd always been the one—other than Will—who could read Enoch best. So he turned his back on his brother, focusing on unhitching the horses from the traces. Yet he could feel James's gaze boring into him, searching and far too perceptive.

"You know this wasn't your fault, right?" James's voice came quiet but firm.

Enoch's jaw clenched. He led the first horse to the hitching rail and reached for a brush.

James followed him with the second gelding. "Accidents happen, Enoch. You can't control everything. Mandie doesn't blame you."

"Maybe she should." The words bit out of him. He moved to brush the animal's other side, keeping his eyes fixed on the task.

"Why? Because you couldn't predict a hidden rut in the road? Because you didn't force her to stay home against her will?" James shook his head. "You're being too hard on yourself."

Enoch ran the brush over a spot of dried mud with more force than necessary. The horse snorted and sidled away from him. He drew a ragged breath, trying to gentle his movements.

"I think we need to find a safer place for Mandie to live. Maybe find a house in town—or build her one."

James huffed out something that sounded almost like a laugh. "You're going to send her away now? Why can't you just admit you love the woman and marry her like any other man would?"

James didn't understand. Somehow Enoch had to make him see.

"I can't go through this again." His voice cracked on the final word, the admission scraping his throat raw. "Losing Charlotte nearly destroyed me. If I get any closer to Mandie and something happens to her..."

James's hand landed on his shoulder. "I know you're scared. After everything you've been through, it's understandable. But you can't let fear control your life. Mandie is fine. Don't push her away because of what might happen."

Enoch shrugged off his brother's touch, his fingers tightening on the brush until his knuckles whitened. "I can't...I won't survive losing someone else I love. It's better not to let myself get too attached in the first place."

James sighed, his breath misting in the cooling air. "Is it really better, though? To hold yourself apart, to never let yourself fully love or be loved, because you're afraid of the pain?"

Enoch's throat constricted. He closed his eyes against the sudden sting of tears. "I don't know. I just...I can't risk it."

He *wanted* to believe his brother. *Wanted* to let himself give in to these feelings for Mandie. But the fear, the memory of shattering grief, held him back like a physical chain.

CHAPTER 24

andie eyed herself in the mirror after dressing for the family's simple church service, in the main room of the Balfour home. She'd donned her blue dress—one of the nicer ones she'd brought with her, though not the very nicest. The extra flounces around the waist on this one concealed her rounding middle better than the others.

She would need to tell James, Robert, and Thomas about her condition soon. If she stayed.

With a sigh, she turned away from the mirror. The past two days since the wagon accident, Enoch had retreated into himself again, even more than after the kiss. This reminded her too much of the brooding shadow he'd been when she first arrived.

If he wouldn't let her in, should she simply leave? She would stay and fight for him if it would help.

But she'd already fought through his defenses twice. The idea of having to do it again felt exhausting. And would he pull back every time the threat of danger touched their lives?

She couldn't… She just couldn't fight to keep her heart intact *and* heal his if he never joined the battle on her side.

If only Bea were here, with her gentle wisdom and knack for soothing ruffled feathers.

Mandie sighed and opened the door of her bed chamber.

Voices drifted from the main room, and she followed the sound to where the Balfour men sat in the main room, Bibles in hand.

Thomas looked up and smiled as she entered. "Ah, Mandie. You're looking pretty in your Sunday finery."

She returned his smile, appreciating his kindness even as her gaze drifted to Enoch.

He sat stiffly in his chair, his eyes fixed on the pages of his Bible. The shadows under them spoke of a restless night, and her heart ached. But she couldn't fix what he wouldn't acknowledge was broken.

"Thank you." She settled onto the sofa beside Thomas, smoothing her skirts. "So, who is leading the service today?"

"I thought I might read the scripture, if no one objects," James said. "And perhaps Robert could lead us in a hymn or two, and Thomas can read the sermon."

Robert nodded. "I'd be happy to. Any requests?"

As the brothers discussed the order of the service, Mandie let her mind wander. She couldn't help but steal glances at Enoch, hoping to catch his eye, to see some hint of the warmth and connection they'd shared before. But he kept his gaze turned away from her.

Finally, James cleared his throat and opened his Bible. "Shall we begin?"

The others murmured their assent, and James started to read, his rich baritone filling the room.

Mandie tried to focus on the familiar words, to let them soothe her heart. But her thoughts kept circling back to Enoch, to the chasm that had opened between them once again.

As the service passed, she had to pull her mind back to the

teaching over and over, like a stubborn horse struggling against the lead rope.

At last, James led them in a closing prayer. It didn't escape her notice that none of them had suggested Enoch take part in the proceedings. Maybe they thought it better to leave the bear alone instead of poking it. But maybe a reminder of God's faithfulness would be good for him.

Of course, she knew better than to attempt to be another's conscience. She couldn't manage to keep herself free of sin, so she'd best let God handle Enoch. *If You could see fit to help him trust You instead of taking the weight for everyone else on his shoulders, that would be good, Lord.*

When James said "amen," Mandie echoed it along with the others.

Silence settled for a moment, then Thomas cleared his throat. "I had a thought. Since we don't have to work, why don't we do something special this afternoon? A fun pastime to lift our spirits."

Robert raised an eyebrow. "What did you have in mind?"

A mischievous twinkle entered Thomas's eyes. "We haven't had a proper dance in ages. And I happen to know that Robert here is a fine hand with the violin."

Mandie widened her eyes. "You play, Robert? I had no idea." The prospect of music and dancing released some of the heaviness in her chest.

Robert ducked his head, a hint of color rising to his cheeks. "It's been a while, but I could manage a few tunes." He glanced around at his brothers.

James grinned. "I think it's a capital idea. We could all use a bit of cheer." He turned to Enoch, who had remained silent throughout the exchange. "What say you? A dance this fine Sunday afternoon?"

Enoch's jaw tightened. For a long moment, he didn't

respond, his gaze fixed on some distant point. Then, slowly, he nodded. "I have no objection."

It wasn't exactly a ringing affirmative, but Mandie would take it. The chance to dance, to perhaps coax a smile from Enoch's stern face, sent a flutter of anticipation through her middle.

"It's settled." Thomas stood. "We'll spruce ourselves up a bit and reconvene in, say, an hour's time?"

The others murmured in agreement and began to disperse to their respective rooms to prepare.

With a sigh, she retreated to her bedchamber and opened her trunk. She fingered the fine fabrics.

She had to lift out the other dresses to reach her best—the deep emerald green gown she'd worn to the Savannah Cotillion last Christmas. The rich color set off her dark hair and eyes, and the cut flattered her figure without being immodest. She had no idea why she would have wasted precious trunk space packing something so impractical for frontier life, but at least she would feel beautiful and confident as she twirled across the makeshift dance floor. She'd brought a few other accessories also—two necklaces, several pairs of gloves, and hairpins and combs.

She laid the dress on the bed and set about freshening up, pinning her hair into a becoming arrangement of curls. By the time she slipped into the gown and managed to fasten the tiny buttons up the back, she felt more like herself than she had in days.

Voices and the tuning of Robert's violin drifted from the main room as she emerged. She paused in the doorway, taking in the scene.

The furniture had been pushed back to the walls, leaving a wide expanse of floor for dancing. Robert stood near the fireplace, violin tucked under his chin as he tested the strings. James and Thomas had changed into suits, and they chatted animatedly as they waited for the festivities to begin.

But it was Enoch who drew her gaze like a lodestone. He stood apart from the others, his broad shoulders filling out his black jacket, underneath it a crisp white shirt and dark trousers. And his face...

She blinked, her breath catching in her throat. He had shaved, the clean lines of his jaw and chin on full display. The effect highlighted the chiseled planes of his features and the startling blue of his eyes.

He looked younger, more vulnerable somehow. And devastatingly handsome.

She'd always known this fact about him. But seeing him like this, polished and gentlemanly, sent a flutter through her middle that had nothing to do with the baby.

As if sensing her stare, he glanced up. Their eyes met, and for a moment, the rest of the room faded away. Something flickered in his blue gaze—surprise, appreciation, perhaps even a flash of the longing she felt.

But then he blinked and the shutters fell, his expression smoothing into the now-familiar mask of detachment.

Thomas let out a whoop, shattering the moment. "There she is, the belle of the ball. Mandie, you look stunning."

Heat rushed to her cheeks as the others turned to her. She smoothed a hand over her skirts. "Thank you, Thomas. You all look quite dashing yourselves."

"Indeed we do." James flashed a grin. "And now that our guest of honor has arrived, I believe it's time for some music. Robert, if you please?"

With a nod, Robert lifted his bow and drew it across the strings in a lively tune. The rollicking notes filled the room, chasing away the lingering shadows.

Thomas stepped forward and sketched a bow before Mandie. "May I have this first dance?"

She managed a smile, placing her fingers in his. "Of course." She'd forgotten gloves. She'd not worn them at all since arriving at the ranch, but a formal occasion such as this should have prompted her memory. They were already dancing though, so she pushed the lack from her thoughts.

He swept her into the center of the room, arranging their hands in the proper positions. As they began to move to the music, Mandie let the familiar steps and cheerful tune wash over her, pushing down the riot of emotions Enoch's gaze had stirred.

The first dance ended, and James claimed her hand for the next, his easy smile and sure steps a welcome distraction. But even as she laughed and twirled, she couldn't help but be aware of Enoch watching from the sidelines, his expression unreadable.

After a lively reel with Robert—while Thomas sang the words and clapped the beat in the absence of the violin—Mandie could barely breathe from all the movement and laughter. She fanned her face with one hand, grinning at the brothers. "I may need to sit the next one out to catch my breath."

"Nonsense." Thomas winked at her. "You're the guest of honor, remember? We can't have you wilting in the corner."

"In that case..." She turned to Enoch, meeting his gaze with a boldness she didn't quite feel. "Lord Balfour, would you do me the honor of this dance?"

For a moment, he simply stared at her, something warring in his eyes. Then, at last, he inclined his head. "As you wish, Mrs. Beaumont."

He stepped forward and took her hand, his fingers warm and callused against her own. A shiver raced up her arm, and her pulse stuttered as he drew her close. Maybe this was why she'd forgotten her gloves.

Robert struck up a slower tune, the gentle strains of a waltz. Enoch's hand settled at her waist, the heat of his touch searing through the satin of her gown. She placed her other hand on his shoulder, letting herself enjoy the solid strength of him beneath the fine fabric.

As they began to move, everything else fell away. The music faded to a distant hum, the room blurring at the edges until there was only Enoch—the warmth of his hold, the sureness of his lead, the intensity of his gaze locked on hers.

She was floating, her feet barely skimming the floor as he guided her through the turns and sways. The heat of his hand on her waist sent tingles racing along her nerve endings, and she leaned into his touch, her body craving more.

For a few blissful minutes, the chasm between them disappeared, bridged by the gentle swell of the music and the way their bodies moved as one.

All too soon, the final notes faded away. Enoch's steps slowed and stilled, though he made no move to release her.

She stared up at him, her breath coming fast and shallow.

His eyes burned into hers, dark with an emotion she couldn't name. His gaze dropped to her lips, and for a wild, reckless moment, he looked like he might kiss her right there in the middle of the room with his brothers watching.

Her lips parted, a silent invitation. She swayed towards him, her body acting of its own volition.

The sound of a wagon outside shattered the moment like a stone through glass.

Enoch blinked, his hands falling away from her as he stepped back. The shutters slammed down over his expression once more.

"Someone's coming." James strode to the door.

Mandie's heart sank as the spell between her and Enoch dissolved completely.

He turned away from her, his jaw set in that familiar, rigid line, and moved toward the window.

James cracked the front door enough to see out. "Looks

like...there's a man and woman. And another man on horseback."

The fine hairs on Mandie's neck prickled, and she hurried to the window beside Enoch. As she peered out at the approaching wagon, her blood turned to ice.

"My parents." The words fell from her lips in a breathless whisper.

And behind them, mounted on a sleek bay gelding, rode Clayton Beaumont.

CHAPTER 25

*M*andie's middle roiled as Enoch's head snapped toward her, his blue eyes sharp with concern. "Who's that with them?"

Her throat closed, making it difficult to speak. "Clayton Beaumont." She forced the name out like a bitter medicine.

Enoch's expression darkened, and his stance shifted—protective, alert. "The one who—"

"Yes." She cut him off. She couldn't hear the words spoken aloud. Her hands trembled as she smoothed her skirts. She had to compose herself before she could face what awaited outside.

The wagon halted in the yard, and her mother descended with her usual regal bearing, her traveling dress immaculate despite the long journey. Her father followed, his weathered face scanning the ranch buildings with obvious disapproval.

Clayton swung down from his horse, still taking in his surroundings. Even from this distance, she could see the satisfied smile playing on his lips. Like a cat who'd cornered a particularly elusive mouse.

"We'll handle this." Enoch's voice carried a note of steel she'd never heard before.

"I need to greet them." She moved toward the door on unsteady legs, though every instinct screamed at her to flee. "They're my parents."

Enoch caught her arm. "You don't have to face him alone."

The simple words steadied her more than any elaborate reassurance could have. She drew a shaking breath and nodded.

They stepped onto the porch together, the other three brothers right behind.

Mandie forced herself to descend the steps, though every instinct screamed at her to flee back into the safety of the house.

"Mandie, darling!" Her mother swept forward, arms outstretched. "Oh, my dear girl, we've been so worried."

Despite everything, her mother's embrace felt good. She'd missed the familiar scent of lavender water and those comforting arms. "Mama. Papa." She turned to include her father, who gathered her into his own fierce hug.

"When you disappeared like that, without a word..." Her father's voice was gruff with emotion. "We feared the worst."

Over her father's shoulder, she caught sight of Clayton approaching, that predatory smile still fixed on his face. Her stomach lurched, and she pulled back from her father.

"What is he doing here?" Her words came out sharp.

Her mother's brow furrowed. "Clayton was worried about you too, dear. When you vanished so suddenly, we all feared for your safety. Without his help, we never would have been able to track you this far."

Clayton stepped closer, removing his hat with an elegant flourish. "Amanda, my dear. You cannot imagine my relief to see you safe and well." His voice carried all the smoothness of honey over broken glass. "I've missed you terribly."

Mandie's skin crawled at the endearment, and she instinctively stepped backward until she reached the solid warmth of Enoch behind her. His presence gave her courage to lift her chin.

"You weren't invited here, Clayton." Her voice carried more strength than she felt. "You need to leave."

Her mother's eyes widened. "Mandie! What's gotten into you? Clayton is practically family. And who is this man?" She gestured toward Enoch with obvious disapproval.

She shifted to the side so she could make introductions. "Mama, Papa, may I present Lord Enoch Balfour?" She motioned to each brother in turn. "And his brothers, Lord James, Lord Robert, and Lord Thomas. I was injured during my journey here, and the Balfour family has graciously taken me in and cared for me."

Then she gestured to her parents. "Gentlemen, my parents. Mr. and Mrs. Theodore Sinclair."

Enoch stepped forward with the polished manners of his noble upbringing. "Mrs. Sinclair. Mr. Sinclair." His tone was perfectly correct, but she caught the underlying tension. Did her parents notice it? "Your daughter has been a welcome guest in our home."

Clayton's smile never wavered, but something cold flickered in his dark eyes as he assessed Enoch. "How fortunate that Mandie found such...hospitable neighbors in this wilderness."

Enoch stiffened the tiniest bit at Clayton's tone. She needed to do something to fix this situation before it turned for the worse.

She frowned at her parents. "Clayton isn't welcome here. He needs to leave *now*."

Her mother's face flushed. "Amanda! I don't know what's come over you, but this rudeness is unacceptable. Clayton is a dear family friend who has done nothing but help us find you."

"He is not a friend." The words tore from her throat, raw with suppressed fury. "Clayton is—"

"Now, now," Clayton interrupted smoothly, his voice dripping false concern. "I can see the journey and your injury have left you overwrought, my dear. We should get you back to that little village where you can rest and collect yourself."

He moved forward as if to take her arm, and Mandie recoiled so hard she nearly stumbled.

Enoch's hand steadied her, then he shifted to place himself between her and Clayton. When he spoke, his voice held a deadly calm. "You heard the lady. You're not welcome here."

Her mother drew herself up. "I'm not sure I care for your friend's manners, Mandie. A true gentleman wouldn't be so discourteous to a guest."

"Clayton is not a good man, Mama." Mandie's voice trembled with the fury that roiled through her. How dare her parents bring that man to her doorstep? And to claim he was helping...

Of course they didn't know the truth. They must not, or they wouldn't have brought him.

Her middle swooped. She needed to tell them. But not everyone together.

Her mother. She had to tell her mother what Clayton had done.

She glanced around. She couldn't do it with all the men watching. Who knew how Mama would react? Yet going inside with her mother and leaving all this fury to face off against each other?

She'd have to chance it. Clayton would be the loser in any battle against all four Balfour brothers, and she couldn't find even a scrap of pity for the lecher.

She stepped back. "Mama, I need to speak with you alone. Inside."

All eyes turned to her, but Enoch's was the only gaze she met. She gave a slight nod to answer the question he no doubt wanted to ask. She was going to tell the truth, as much of it as she knew.

"Perhaps we could all come inside rather than waiting on

your doorstep." Clayton spoke in that patronizing tone that clearly insinuated the Balfours possessed no hospitality. He was simply trying to protect himself though. He'd no doubt pretend Mandie had lost her mind and was spouting nonsense.

"No." Enoch nearly growled the word, and he took a step forward, blocking Clayton's path to the porch steps.

Her mother glanced at her father, then sighed and moved to follow Mandie into the house. "I hope you have a proper explanation for all this."

Mandie's heart hammered against her ribs as she led her mother through the front door and into the main room. The remnants of their cheerful afternoon—pushed-back furniture, Robert's violin case open on the mantel—seemed to mock the gravity of what she was about to reveal.

Her mother's sharp gaze took in the polished wood floors, the fine furnishings, the obvious prosperity of the household. Some of the disapproval in her expression eased. "Well. They do seem to live quite respectably for being so far from civilization."

"Mama, please sit down." Mandie gestured toward the sofa, her hands trembling. How did one begin such a conversation? How did one tell her mother that a man she'd welcomed into their home, trusted with her daughter's welfare, was a monster?

Her mother perched on the edge of the cushions, her back ramrod straight. "Now then, what is this nonsense about Clayton? He's been nothing but helpful these past months, searching for you, comforting your father and me. The man was beside himself with worry."

The words churned a new round of fury inside her. Clayton, comforting her parents? Playing the concerned suitor while she fled across the country to escape him? The calculated cruelty of it stole her breath.

"He forced himself on me." The words burst out like a dam breaking, raw and terrible in the quiet afternoon air.

Her mother's face went ashen, one hand flying to her throat. "Mandie, surely you're mistaken. Clayton would never—"

"I'm not mistaken." The words came out harder than she intended, but she couldn't soften them. Not when her mother's first instinct was to doubt her. "And I'm…" She couldn't get these words out. But she had to. "I'm…with child."

Her mother stared at her, mouth opening and closing like a fish gasping for air. The color had drained completely from her cheeks.

"But…but he's been so kind. So helpful in the search for you." Her mother's voice was barely a whisper. "He even funded the journey here."

A bitter laugh escaped Mandie's throat. "Of course he did. He wasn't helping *you* find me. *He* wants me. My…" She slashed her hand through the air. "Nicholas's money. Everything. He tried to make me marry him, but when I turned him away, he…"

Her mother straightened, and she exhaled a long breath. "I… I can't believe it. Surely there's a misunderstanding."

"Misunderstanding?" Mandie's voice cracked, and she pressed her hands to her stomach protectively. "There's no misunderstanding. He forced himself on me, and now I'm with child." Even faced with the truth, her mother still wanted to find an excuse for Clayton's behavior.

Her mother's face crumpled, and for the first time since Mandie could remember, she looked fragile. Old. "Oh, my dear girl. Why didn't you come to us? Why didn't you tell your father?"

"Would Papa have believed me? Against Clayton's word?" Mandie's laugh held no humor. "You're already taking his side against me."

The truth of those words hung heavy between them. Her mother's hands twisted in her lap, and Mandie saw the moment understanding truly dawned—not just of what Clayton had done, but of why her daughter had felt she had no choice but to flee.

"The baby…" her mother whispered.

"Is Clayton's, yes." Mandie lifted her chin, daring her mother to pass judgment. "And he will never, ever get his hands on either of us."

Outside, raised voices filtered through the windows—her father's gruff tones, Clayton's smooth replies, then the steel-edged warning in Enoch's voice. Her heart lurched.

She needed to get back out there before the men came to blows.

CHAPTER 26

*E*very muscle in Enoch's body coiled like a spring, ready to snap at this skunk who'd dared step foot on their property. Who'd dared force his presence on Mandie again.

The only thing keeping him from launching himself at Clayton and beating the smug expression off his face was the fact that Mandie needed to handle this her way—at least until her parents understood what kind of blackguard they'd brought to his doorstep.

The front door opened behind him, and Enoch swung around as Mandie's mother charged outside. Mandie followed close on her heels, her voice a desperate murmur that her mother appeared to be ignoring.

"Mama, please."

But her mother had already positioned herself on the porch like a queen addressing her subjects, arms folded across her chest. Her sharp gaze swept over the assembled men before settling on her husband.

"Theodore." Her voice cut through the afternoon air like a blade. "Amanda has just informed me that Clayton forced himself on her, and she is now carrying his child."

180

The words hit the yard like a thunderclap, and for a heartbeat, no one moved. Even the mountain breeze stilled. He'd forgotten his brothers didn't know about Mandie's condition.

He wanted to see Mandie's reaction, but Clayton felt like the bigger threat just now.

The cad's expression shifted seamlessly into one of pained surprise, his hand moving to his heart as if wounded by the very suggestion. "Mrs. Sinclair, I'm devastated that Amanda would make such an accusation. I can only imagine how the grief and isolation have affected her judgment. Her injuries too."

His voice carried the perfect note of hurt confusion. "I fear her grief over Nicholas has affected her mind more than we realized. I know she's been...fragile. She spoke often of her regret that she never gave Nicholas a son to carry on the Beaumont name."

He paused, allowing his voice to catch with what seemed like genuine emotion. "I tried to comfort her, as any family member would. Perhaps...perhaps in her fragile state, she misunderstood my intentions. And now, faced with the reality of carrying a child out of wedlock, she needs someone to blame."

His eyes glistened with what appeared to be tears. "I can't say I begrudge her. The shame must be overwhelming." He cleared his throat and turned to Mandie's father. "I would be willing to marry her. To give the babe a father and cover any hint of scandal."

Enoch's jaw clenched. The snake was smooth. He'd give him that.

Mrs. Sinclair's gaze swung back to Mandie, who stood wrapped in her own arms, looking small and vulnerable against the door frame. The sight of her like that—alone and doubted even by her own parents—made Enoch want to stride up those steps and pull her against his side.

"Amanda." Her mother's voice came gentler now, but also carried an edge of doubt. "We can discuss all of this on the way home. Perhaps you can stay with your cousin Margaret at the plantation in the country until after the baby arrives. No one need know there was any...irregularity. We can smooth this over."

The words hit Enoch like a physical blow. They were going to sweep this under a rug and ship Mandie off to hide her shame—while Clayton walked free. The injustice of it sent fire racing through his veins.

But it was Mandie's reaction that twisted his gut. She looked...hesitant. As if she might actually be considering their offer. The thought made something cold and desperate claw at his chest.

Did she *want* to go with them? These people who'd brought her attacker straight to her, who questioned her word even now?

But they were her parents. Her family.

No matter how poorly they'd protected her, blood ties ran deep. He understood that pull—the desperate need to belong somewhere, to be wanted by the people who should love you the most.

"I..." Mandie's voice was barely audible. "I don't know."

Clayton stepped forward, his expression the picture of wounded nobility. "Amanda, my dear, if I've somehow given you the wrong impression—"

"Stay back." The words tore from Enoch's throat before he could stop them. He moved to block Clayton's path completely, every instinct screaming at him to protect what was his.

Except she wasn't his. And if she chose to leave with them, she never would be.

The realization hit him like a physical blow. He'd spent so much time building walls to protect himself from loss that he'd never allowed himself to consider what he might be losing by keeping her at arm's length. James had tried to tell him. Now— when it might be too late—he finally had to face his loss.

James stepped up beside him, his own expression grim. "Perhaps we should let Mandie make her own decision without pressure from anyone."

Clayton's mask slipped for just an instant, revealing a flash of irritation before the concerned expression returned. "Of course. Though I think we can all agree that Amanda needs the support of her family during this difficult time."

"Support?" Enoch spat the word. "Is that what you call bringing her attacker to her refuge?"

Mr. Sinclair finally spoke, his weathered face creased with confusion and growing anger. "Now see here, young man. I don't know what game you're playing, but Clayton is—"

"A liar and a villain." Enoch's voice cut through the man's words like a sword. He was done with politeness, done with letting that snake charm his way out of consequences. "Your daughter fled halfway across the country to escape him, and you brought him right to her."

Clayton's face flushed with righteous indignation. "Sir, I must protest this slanderous—"

"Protest all you want." Robert moved to flank Enoch's other side, his usually gentle demeanor replaced by something far more dangerous. "But we've seen what your presence does to Mandie. That's all the proof we need."

Thomas stepped forward as well, completing the wall of Balfour brothers between Clayton and the porch. "Seems to me a real gentleman would respect a lady's wishes and leave when asked."

Clayton's composure finally cracked, his charming mask slipping to reveal the cold calculation beneath. His sneer swept over the four of them. "How touching. The lady found herself some frontier protectors." His lips curved. "But this is a family matter, and Amanda will come to her senses once she's away from whatever influence you've exerted over her."

"The only influence we've exerted"—Enoch kept his voice

steady—"is showing her what it means to be treated with respect."

Mandie's sharp intake of breath drew every eye. She stood straighter now, her chin lifted with a resolve that made Enoch's chest tighten with pride and fear in equal measure. When she spoke, her voice carried across the yard with crystal clarity.

"I'm not leaving here." She descended the porch steps slowly, her emerald dress rustling with each measured movement. "I won't hide away on some plantation to spare the family from scandal."

Her mother's face went pale. "Amanda, be reasonable. Think of your reputation. Think of the child."

"I am thinking of my child." Mandie's hand moved to cover her middle. "Which is why I won't put either of us anywhere near him."

Her gaze fixed on Clayton with unmistakable revulsion. "You want to know the truth? Clayton cornered me in my parlor and insisted I marry him. When I refused his proposal, he forced himself on me on the very sofa where my husband used to read his evening papers."

The raw honesty in her voice cut through the afternoon air like a blade.

Clayton's face went ashen, then flushed dark red.

"Amanda, please," her mother whispered.

"No." Mandie's voice grew stronger with each word. "I won't be silent anymore. I won't let him twist this into some story about my grief or fragile feminine sensibilities. He violated me, and now he has the audacity to stand here and offer to marry me as if he were some noble savior."

Enoch had never been prouder of anyone in his life than Mandie in that moment. She possessed a strength he could only dream of. And she made him want to be a man who deserved her. At the very least, he would lay down his life to protect her.

He turned back to Clayton. "You'd better mount that horse now and get off our property, or you'll be escorted at gunpoint."

Clayton's face twisted, the mask of gentility finally dropping completely. "You think these mountain savages can protect you forever, Amanda? You're carrying *my* child. *My* heir. That gives me rights—"

"You have no rights here." Mr. Sinclair's voice boomed across the yard, silencing every other sound. Mandie's father stepped forward, his weathered face carved from granite. "Get away from my daughter. Now."

Gone was the confused, uncertain man of moments before. In his place stood someone Enoch recognized—a father whose child had been attacked.

The fury in Clayton's eyes burned hot now, all pretense abandoned. "You'll regret this, Theodore. All of you." His gaze swept the assembled group with venomous promise. "That child is a Beaumont, and I'll have what's mine."

"The only thing you'll have is a bullet if you don't get off our land." Enoch's hand moved toward his hip, though he wore no gun belt on this peaceful Sunday afternoon.

Clayton's nostrils flared, but he was outnumbered and he knew it. With jerky movements, he jammed his hat back on his head and stalked toward his horse. "This isn't over, Amanda. A man doesn't forget what belongs to him."

"Nothing here belongs to you." Mandie's voice rang with even more strength. "And it never will."

Clayton swung into his saddle with far more violence than grace, wheeling his horse around to face them one last time. "We'll see about that." He spurred his mount and thundered out of the yard, leaving a cloud of dust and the echo of hoofbeats in his wake.

The silence that followed felt fragile, like glass that might shatter at the slightest touch.

CHAPTER 27

$\mathcal{E}$noch kept his eyes fixed on the dust cloud until it disappeared beyond the tree line, every muscle still coiled for action. Only when the last echo of hoofbeats faded did he allow himself to turn toward Mandie.

She stood frozen on the bottom step, her face pale as winter snow. The fierce strength that had carried her through the confrontation seemed to drain away all at once, leaving her swaying like a sapling in a strong wind.

"Mandie." He moved toward her, but her mother reached her first.

"Oh, my darling girl." Mrs. Sinclair's voice broke as she gathered her daughter into her arms. "I'm so sorry. So very sorry we didn't believe you immediately."

Mr. Sinclair approached more slowly, his weathered hands trembling as he reached out to touch his daughter's shoulder. "Amanda, forgive an old fool. I should have seen…should have known." His voice cracked. "What kind of father brings his daughter's attacker to her very door?"

"You didn't know, Papa." Mandie's words came muffled

against her mother's shoulder. "How could you have known when I never told you?"

"Because it was my job to protect you." The anguish in her father's voice made Enoch's chest tighten. "Instead, I failed you completely."

Enoch watched the family reunion with a growing hollow ache in his chest. This was what Mandie needed—her parents' love.

Their acceptance and protection. Not some emotionally guarded mountain man who couldn't bring himself to tell her how he felt.

"We'll take you home, darling. Away from all this wilderness and danger. You'll be safe with us." Mrs. Sinclair murmured the words as she stroked Mandie's hair.

"No." Mandie pulled back from her mother's embrace, her voice firm despite the tears tracking down her cheeks. "I told you—I'm not leaving."

Her father's brow furrowed. "But, sweetheart, you can't stay here. These men have been kind, but you need proper care. A woman in your condition—"

"I have proper care." Mandie's gaze swept across his brothers before settling on Enoch. Something in her eyes made his breath catch. "I have people who believe me. Who protect me. Who..." She faltered, color rising in her cheeks.

"Who what, darling?" her mother asked gently.

Mandie straightened her shoulders, and when she spoke again, her voice carried a quiet certainty that sent Enoch's heart hammering against his ribs.

"Who see me exactly as I am. Who I love."

The words hung in the mountain air like a challenge and a promise all at once.

They found their mark in Enoch's chest, piercing through every wall he'd built to keep her at arm's length.

She loved him.

The knowledge blazed through him like wildfire, burning away his thickly constructed defenses. Standing there in her emerald dress with tears still wet on her cheeks, she was the most beautiful thing he'd ever seen.

His throat constricted. She was offering him everything he'd ever wanted and all he'd convinced himself he couldn't have. The chance to build something real. To be the man who stood beside her through whatever storms came.

But what if he failed her like he'd failed everyone else? What if his attempts to protect her only brought more danger to her door?

Mrs. Sinclair followed her daughter's gaze to Enoch, her eyebrows rising with sudden understanding. "I see." She studied him with the calculating assessment of a mother weighing her daughter's suitor. "And do you return my daughter's feelings, Lord Balfour?"

Every eye turned to him, waiting. His brothers wore expressions of barely contained hope.

Mr. Sinclair looked skeptical but not hostile.

Mrs. Sinclair appeared to be dissecting his very soul.

But it was Mandie who mattered. Mandie, who stood there with her heart in her eyes, having just laid her feelings bare before God and everyone. She deserved his honesty, even if the truth terrified him.

"I do." The words came out rougher than he intended. "More than I ever thought possible. More than I know what to do with." He swallowed hard, his gaze never leaving hers. "She's the bravest, strongest woman I've ever known, and I'd count myself the most fortunate man alive if she'd have me."

The admission hung between them like a bridge waiting to be crossed. Mandie's eyes widened, hope and wonder chasing across her features.

"Then ask her properly." Mrs. Sinclair's voice broke through the bubble of Mandie's response. "A woman in my daughter's condition needs the security of marriage, sir. Not pretty words."

Heat crawled up Enoch's neck. He'd never imagined proposing marriage with an audience of five, but perhaps it was fitting. Mandie deserved witnesses to his commitment—people who would hold him accountable if he failed her.

He stepped closer, close enough to see the gold flecks in her brown eyes. "Amanda Beaumont." His voice came steadier now, weighted with certainty. "Would you do me the honor of becoming my wife?"

"Enoch." His name was barely a whisper on her lips. "Are you certain? The baby—"

"Will be our child." The words came without hesitation. "Blood doesn't make a family, Mandie. Love does. And I already love that little one because he or she is part of you."

A sob escaped her throat, and she pressed her hands to her mouth. "Yes." She spoke through her tears. "Of course, yes."

He reached for her then, and she melted against him. The rightness of it settled into his bones—the way she fit against his chest, the way her tears dampened his shirt, the way her arms wrapped around him as if she'd never let him go.

"Thank you." He pressed his mouth close to her ear so only she would hear his whisper. "For trusting me with your heart. For staying. For being brave enough to fight when I was too much of a coward to join the battle."

"You're here now," she whispered back. "That's all that matters."

"Well." Mrs. Sinclair's voice carried a note of approval that surprised him. "I suppose if my daughter must live in this wilderness, at least she'll have a proper husband to look after her."

Mr. Sinclair cleared his throat. "You'll forgive a father's concern, Lord Balfour, but what are your intentions regarding my daughter's...situation? There will be talk, no matter how quickly you marry."

Enoch lifted his head to meet the older man's gaze directly. "Let them talk. Anyone who has a problem with my wife or our child will answer to me." The steel in his voice left no room for doubt. "As far as I'm concerned, this baby is a blessing, not a burden."

Mrs. Sinclair gave a firm nod. "Under the circumstances, I think a simple ceremony would be most appropriate. Perhaps next week? We could arrange for the minister from town."

"No." Mandie lifted her head from Enoch's shoulder, her voice firm. "I don't want to wait. Not when Clayton might..." She shuddered.

Enoch tightened his arms around her. She was right—the sooner they were married, the sooner she'd have the legal protection of his name. "We could ride to Walnut Springs tomorrow. Find the preacher there."

Mr. Sinclair cleared his throat. "If you're certain this is what you want, Amanda. This man—" He studied Enoch with the shrewd gaze of a father protecting his daughter. "You'll provide for her? Protect her?"

"With my life, sir." Enoch met the older man's stare without flinching. "Your daughter means everything to me. I'd die before I let harm come to her."

Something in Mr. Sinclair's expression softened at the raw honesty in Enoch's voice. "Then you have my blessing." He extended his weathered hand, and Enoch clasped it. "Though I reserve the right to shoot you if you ever make her cry."

A startled laugh escaped Mandie's throat. "Papa!"

"What? A man's got to look after his little girl." Mr. Sinclair's gruff tone couldn't hide the moisture gathering in his eyes.

Mrs. Sinclair dabbed at her own eyes with a lace handkerchief. "Well then, we have a wedding to plan. Amanda, you'll need a proper dress, and we'll have to see about flowers and—"

"Mama." Mandie raised a hand, stilling her planning. "I don't need all that. I just need him." Her gaze found Enoch's again, and the simple truth in her words made his chest tighten.

"But darling, it's your wedding day. Surely you want—"

"I want to be his wife." The quiet certainty in Mandie's voice silenced any further protests. "Everything else is just…decoration."

CHAPTER 28

The soft murmur of her parents' voices drifted from behind her as Mandie stepped onto the porch, breathing in the crisp mountain air that had become as essential to her as prayer itself.

"They've finally settled in?" Enoch's voice came from the shadows near the porch rail, and her heart did that familiar skip that always came when he spoke.

"Mama's making lists for tomorrow, and Papa's questioning Robert about the economics of a ranch business." She moved toward him, letting herself take in the way the lamplight from the great room windows caught the strong line of his jaw. "I think they're still adjusting to the idea that their daughter lives in what Mama calls *the untamed wilderness.*"

A smile tugged at the corner of his mouth. "And what do you call it?"

"Home." The word slipped out before she could catch it, carrying more weight than she'd intended. Heat crept up her neck, but Enoch's expression softened in a way that made her chest flutter.

The mountains were home, but what about England? Should

she have said something to her parents? Asked Enoch about it? They'd spoken little about it of late, but eventually, they would both need to travel there. Even live there?

Before she could decide whether to mention it, Enoch nodded toward the pasture. "Willow and the foal need to come in for the night. Want to walk with me?"

"Yes." The answer came without hesitation, and she fell into step beside him as they made their way down the porch steps and across the yard.

They'd had almost no time alone since his very public proposal earlier, and it would be wonderful just to be with him. In this place, with these animals they both loved.

The evening air carried the scent of pine and the distant sound of the creek bubbling over stones. Above them, the first stars were beginning to pierce the deepening sky. This felt so different from the carefully orchestrated evening strolls of her Richmond days.

This was real. Unguarded. True.

Willow lifted her head as they approached and nickered in greeting.

"There's my girl." Mandie reached out to stroke the mare's velvet nose. The foal pressed close to Willow's side, still cautious but no longer skittish around them.

Enoch slipped a rope around the mare's neck, then opened the gate and led her toward the barn.

The foal's legs still seemed too long for her body, but she moved with increasing confidence, her coat gleaming silver in the moonlight.

"She's grown so much already," Mandie murmured as they secured the horses in their stall. She couldn't resist running her hand along the foal's neck one more time before Enoch latched the gate.

"Growing fast."

They stood at the stall gate, watching the mare nuzzle her

offspring. The familiar ache of longing tightened in her chest—by spring, she would have her own baby to nurture and protect. Would she know instinctively how to care for her baby as Willow had?

A new thought slipped in, sending a surge of panic through her. England…would she have to give birth in a strange country?

"What's wrong?" Somehow Enoch must have felt her fear.

She couldn't quite make herself meet his gaze, especially with the furrows shadowing his brow. "I was just…wondering. You haven't said much about England, though I know we'll need to travel there. I wasn't sure if it would be before…"

He must have understood her meaning, for he reached out to touch the back of her arm. His thumb stroked up and down that sensitive skin, and her sleeve did nothing to stop a tingle sliding over her skin. "I plan to tell my father it will be at least a year before we can come, perhaps longer. That way, you can choose where you'd like to have the baby. And you'll both have as much time as you want to recover. To grow strong and healthy."

The warmth of his gaze heated her cheek, and she finally made herself turn to him. To meet his eyes. The open roof of the barn allowed moonlight in so she could see their navy intensity.

"Thank you." The words didn't seem nearly enough. "That…would be nice."

"Nice." He stepped closer, close enough that she could see the way his eyes crinkled at the corners. "My wife calls having our baby wherever she chooses *nice*." The word rolled off his tongue with gentle teasing, but underneath lay something deeper. Something that made her pulse quicken.

"Your wife." She tested the words, letting them settle on her tongue like honey. "I'm still getting used to that word." Especially the wife of *this* man.

"Are you having second thoughts?" The question came quietly, but she caught the thread of vulnerability in his tone.

"No." She turned fully toward him. "Never. It's just…this morning I woke up a widow hiding from her past. Tonight I'm going to sleep as a woman engaged to marry the man she loves." The admission slipped out before she could stop it. But she didn't want to take the words back.

Something shifted in his expression—like a wall crumbling. "The man she loves." He repeated the words like she had, as if testing them.

"Yes." She lifted her chin, letting him see the truth in her eyes. "I know I said it earlier, in front of everyone, but I wanted you to hear it when it's just us. I love you, Enoch Balfour. Not because you're protecting me, or because you're willing to claim my child as your own, though those things mean more than I can say." Her voice cracked, and she had to pause.

She had to find the right words to help him see who he really was. "I love you because you're good and loyal and faithful. You're a man of integrity. Of faith. You make me feel safe. When I'm with you, I feel like the woman I was meant to be. You see *me*—not the role I'm supposed to play or the expectations I'm supposed to meet—but the real me."

The moonlight caught the moisture gathering in his eyes, and her heart clenched at the raw emotion there.

His hand came up to cup her cheek, his thumb brushing across her skin with reverent gentleness. "Mandie." Her name was barely a whisper on his lips.

She let her eyes sink closed, leaning into his touch. "I was so afraid that what happened with Clayton had broken something in me. That I'd never be able to trust a man's hands on me again. But with you…" She covered his hand with hers, pressing it more firmly against her face. "With you, I feel safe. Cherished."

"You are cherished." His words came rough with emotion. "More than you know. More than I've been brave enough to tell you." His other hand found her waist, drawing her closer. "I've spent so many years convinced I was better off alone. That caring for someone meant inevitable loss."

"And now?" She opened her eyes so she didn't miss whatever his eyes wanted to tell her.

"Now I realize the only real loss would be letting you slip away because I was too much a coward to fight for what we could have together." His forehead touched hers, and his warm breath brushed her lips.

She let her hands rest on his chest, on the steady rhythm of his heartbeat.

"I love you too, Amanda Beaumont." He tightened his hold at her waist. "Love your strength, your courage, the way you see beauty in this wild place that's become my sanctuary. You are extraordinary." His voice dropped to a whisper. "And I'm terrified."

"Of marrying me?" Her insides tightened, and she started to pull back to better see his face.

He held her steady as he shook his head. "Of being this happy."

She eased out a breath, letting her nerves uncoil again.

"I keep waiting for something to destroy it. Some disaster to prove I don't deserve this." His thumb traced along her jawline. "But then I look at you, and I think maybe…maybe God means for us to have this. Maybe all the pain and loss led us both here, to each other."

"Maybe it did." She couldn't help but smile as the idea formed shape in her mind. "Maybe that's what healing looks like —not the absence of scars, but the beauty in their final form."

His breath caught, and for a moment they simply stood there in the moonlight, foreheads touching, sharing the same air.

Willow shifted in her stall, and somewhere in the distance, an owl hooted through the pines.

Enoch spoke first, his voice a husky murmur. "Tomorrow, you'll be my wife."

She breathed out a smile. "Tomorrow, you'll be my husband."

The words settled between them like a promise, and now the space separating their lips felt unbearable.

She rose on her toes at the same moment he lowered his head, and when their mouths met, the tenderness weakened her knees.

The kiss deepened slowly, his hands threading through her hair as hers fisted in the fabric of his shirt. This wasn't the desperate, urgent embrace of their first kiss, when they'd both been fighting against what they felt. Instead, it carried the weight of promises made and fears conquered. His lips moved against hers with gentle reverence, as if she were something precious he'd been entrusted to protect.

When he finally eased back, they both breathed heavy. Enoch rested his chin against the top of her head, and she sank against his chest, where the rapid beat of his heart thudded against her cheek. The solid warmth of him anchored her to this moment, to this life she'd chosen.

"We should go back." He made no move to release her though. "Your parents will wonder where you are."

"In a moment." She wasn't ready for this peace to end, this perfect bubble of contentment that surrounded them here.

Tomorrow would bring the ride to town, the ceremony, the reality of becoming his wife. Tonight, she simply wanted to exist in this space between promise and fulfillment.

A coyote's distant howl drifted across the valley, answered by another from the opposite ridge. The sound should have been haunting, perhaps even frightening, but here in Enoch's arms, it felt like a benediction—the wild country's blessing on their union.

CHAPTER 29

$\mathcal{D}$awn painted the eastern peaks in shades of rose and gold, but Mandie had been awake long before the sun crested the mountains. Her heart hammered with a mixture of anticipation and nervous energy that made sleep impossible.

Today she would become Mrs. Enoch Balfour.

Or…Lady Balfour? That didn't feel right. *Enoch's wife* would be more than enough.

Someone had already built up the fire in the stove when she stepped into the kitchen. Probably Enoch. The water in the kettle was almost hot as well.

She would prepare an easy meal this morning. The cornbread batter came together quickly, followed by thick slices of ham that sizzled in the cast iron skillet. The rhythm of cooking helped settle her nerves, grounding her in simple, necessary tasks while her mind spun with everything the day would bring.

The eggs cracked clean against the bowl's rim, their golden yolks sliding into the mixture as she whisked them.

Outside, the low murmur of men's voices rose—the brothers discussing their plans for the day, no doubt.

Footsteps in the dining room drew her attention, and her

mother appeared in the doorway, already dressed despite the early hour. Dark circles shadowed her eyes, suggesting she'd slept as poorly as Mandie.

"Good morning, dear." Mama's voice carried a tremor of emotion. "I thought I might help with breakfast."

"The ham just needs turning in a few minutes." Mandie poured the eggs into another skillet, watching them foam and set at the edges. "Did you sleep at all?"

Her mother moved to stand beside her, hands fluttering uncertainly before settling on the counter. "Some. I kept thinking about your first wedding." She paused, her voice growing thick. "The church full of flowers and all our friends, your father walking you down the aisle in that beautiful gown we had commissioned…"

Her tone dropped and sadness crept in. "And now here you are in a frontier kitchen, preparing to marry a man we barely know, in such a…rough ceremony." Mama's voice caught.

Mandie set down her wooden spoon and turned to face her mother fully. "My marriage with Nicholas was…acceptable." She couldn't summon a better word to describe the mixture of companionship and loneliness. She'd thought she'd managed to grow love for him, yet compared to the way she felt about Enoch…

"But Mama, what I feel for Enoch is so much more than I ever imagined possible. That beautiful church wedding you remember? I was terrified the entire time. Terrified of disappointing Nicholas, of not being the wife he expected, of living my whole life trying to fit into a mold that never quite suited me."

Her mother's eyes widened, and Mandie reached for her hands.

"Today I'm nervous, yes, but not afraid. Not the way I was before. Enoch sees me—truly sees me—and loves what he finds.

That's worth more than all the flowers and fancy gowns in Savannah."

Tears gathered in her mother's eyes as she nodded. "It is. I just…I want everything to be perfect for you."

"It will be perfect because it's right." Mandie squeezed her mother's hands. "A simple ceremony with the people we love most—that sounds far more beautiful to me than any elaborate affair."

The sound of boots and voices in the great room interrupted them. The brothers had come inside, their conversation low but urgent.

Mama gasped. "The ham." She released Mandie's hands to rescue the skillet before the meat burned.

Mandie turned the eggs one final time before sliding them onto a platter, then carried it to the dining room where the men had gathered around the table—Enoch, his brothers, and even her father.

"Morning." Enoch rose to take the platter from her hands, his fingers brushing hers in the exchange. The brief contact sent warmth up her hands, and she caught the tender look in his eyes before he turned to set the dish on the table. "You look beautiful this morning."

The simple compliment, spoken quietly enough that only she could hear, made her cheeks warm. She would dress for their wedding later, but for now, she'd braided her hair in a simple plait that hung over her shoulder, and wore her everyday blue calico dress. Nothing fancy. Yet the way Enoch looked at her made her insides heat.

Her mother appeared with the ham and cornbread, setting both on the table before taking her seat.

Once they were all settled, Enoch bowed his head to ask the Lord's blessing over the food and the day. His hand found Mandie's under the table as he began the prayer, and the warmth of his palm against hers, his fingers woven through hers, helped settle her insides.

Thank You, Lord, for this man.

At the *amen*, the family began loading plates, and Enoch's voice lowered as he spoke to her, though everyone at the table could hear. "James and Robert will ride ahead to town. Make sure everything's quiet."

"Quiet?" Mama's fork paused halfway to her mouth.

"Just a precaution." James offered the words in a casual tone, but Mandie well knew his meaning.

Her stomach tightened, though she tried to keep her expression neutral. She wouldn't let fear overshadow this day—not when she'd finally found something worth celebrating.

"And I'll head south to fetch Mrs. Wang from the Jenkins' place." Thomas grinned. "She'd never forgive us if we let her miss this day."

"Mrs. Wang?" Mama looked confused.

"Our housekeeper." Enoch's tone carried the warmth reserved for family. "She's been with us since we lived in England. More of a mother to us than a housekeeper, really."

"Oh." Mama's expression softened. "Of course she should be there."

"What time should we plan to leave for town?" Papa cut his ham with methodical precision.

Enoch looked to her, his expression softening in the way it only did when he looked at her. "How much time would you like this morning? I'm planning to rent a room at the boarding house so you have a place to..." Red crept up his neck, and he seemed to lose his words. "...get ready or do whatever you like before..."

She had to bite her lip to keep back a grin at his floundering. "That sounds wonderful. With the room there, I only need an hour or so here before we leave."

She'd wait to dress in town so she didn't soil her gown on the ride.

After only a few more minutes, Robert pushed back from the table. "We should get moving if we want to be back in time. Sun's full up now."

James nodded, rising as well. "We'll send word if anything is amiss, but I expect all will be well."

Thomas stood next, draining the last of his coffee. "I'll collect Mrs. Wang and meet you all in town." His teeth flashed in that charming grin he kept at the ready. "She'll likely box my ears for not coming to get her straightaway after all the excitement yesterday."

The warmth in his voice made Mandie's chest tighten. "Tell her I can't wait to see her." In only a few days, Bea had become such a good friend.

The three brothers filed out, leaving behind a quiet that felt heavy with anticipation.

"Well then." Papa cleared his throat, setting down his napkin. "I suppose that leaves us to prepare for the day." He glanced toward Enoch, who was finishing the last of his eggs. "Perhaps you could put me to work. Maybe hitching the wagon, or whatever else is needed. I can handle a horse well enough."

Enoch looked up from his plate, surprise flickering across his features before settling into something warmer. "I'd appreciate the help. I was planning to put a second bench in the wagon bed so we can all ride together comfortably."

"Good thinking." Papa stood, seeming relieved to have a task. "Lead the way."

The two men rose from the table, and watching them head toward the door left a bittersweet ache in her middle. Perhaps her father would use the time to get to know the man she was marrying—really know him, not just the titles and inheritance that already seemed to fascinate him so.

"Come along, dear." Mama's voice drew her attention back.

"We should get your things packed. Leave these dishes and I'll work on them in a minute. I thought you might like to wear my green silk with the ivory trim. It's not a proper wedding gown, but it's the finest dress we have."

The next hour passed in a blur of hearing Mama's suggestions and nudging them in a direction more appropriate to the setting and what they would be able to accomplish in a short time at the rented room in Walnut Springs. As thankful as she was to have a place in town to freshen up and dress for the ceremony, she didn't plan to keep Enoch waiting an instant longer than she had to.

When they all set out in the wagon, the late summer sun had climbed high enough to warm the mountain air.

Mandie settled beside her mother on the rear bench. Papa took the front bench beside Enoch, and she couldn't help but notice how her father's posture had relaxed since breakfast. Time with Enoch must have been good for him.

"Fine team you have here." Papa started the conversation as Enoch guided the horses down the winding mountain road. "Matched bays—good bone structure, well-trained."

"Thank you, sir. Both were born here on the ranch." Enoch's voice held a proper amount of respect, but she could hear the hint of effort in his tone. He wasn't accustomed to as much conversation as her father could manage.

Papa nodded approvingly. "Breeding your own stock—that's the mark of a well-run operation. I imagine the bloodlines go back to England?"

"Some, yes. My father shipped several mares and a stallion when we first came to Montana." Enoch kept his attention on the road ahead, but Mandie caught the slight tightening around his eyes at the mention of his father. Or maybe England. "We've added local stock as well—horses bred for mountain work."

"Smart approach. Combining the best of both worlds." Papa settled back against the bench, warming to his subject. "And I understand you'll inherit a dukedom eventually? That must weigh on a man's mind, knowing such responsibility awaits."

Mandie's stomach clenched. This was exactly the sort of conversation she'd hoped to avoid today. Her mother leaned forward slightly, no doubt eager to hear Enoch's response.

"It does." Enoch's answer came measured.

"But surely you'll need to return to England soon? To prepare, to take your place in society?" Papa's tone carried the assumption of someone who understood such obligations well.

The wagon jolted over a particularly rough section of road, and Mandie gripped the bench to steady herself. The movement gave her an excuse to catch Enoch's eye when he glanced back to check on them.

She offered him a small smile, but the tense line of his shoulders didn't soften.

He turned back to the road. "Eventually, yes." His jaw tightened almost imperceptibly. "But we'll wait until Mandie and the baby are both ready for travel. My father has given me leave to plan the timing."

"Of course, of course." Papa waved a dismissive hand. "But a man of your station has duties that can't be put off long. The estate, the tenants, parliament—these things require attention."

When Mama spoke, her voice sounded bright with curiosity. "Will Mandie need to be presented at court? I imagine there are certain expectations for a duchess."

The questions pelted like hail, and Mandie's insides knotted as tight as the line of Enoch's shoulders.

She cleared her throat. "Perhaps we could save such discussions for another day? Today feels like a time for celebrating what's ahead, not worrying about distant obligations."

Her mother patted her hand. "Mandie's right. Though I must say, the thought of my daughter as a duchess..." Mama's voice carried a note of wonder mixed with pride. "It's almost too much to fathom."

"Mama." Mandie laced her tone with a warning.

Enoch's quick glance back flashed gratitude in those warm blue eyes.

They'd traveled perhaps an hour—the latter part filled with blessed quiet as her parents took in the beauty around them—when one of the horses nickered and Enoch's head snapped up, his whole body going alert.

A horse and rider appeared around the bend, approaching at a steady trot. James.

Enoch reined in the team, and James halted his mount ahead of them since the trail wasn't wide enough for him to come alongside.

"All quiet in town. We asked around, and no one's seen him since you all came through the first time." He nodded to Mandie's parents, then focused back on Enoch. "Robert stayed to keep an eye on things, just to be sure."

"Good." Enoch nodded, though his grip on the reins didn't relax. "Thomas there yet?"

James shook his head. "Not yet, but it's still early. Should be along soon."

Enoch nodded, then focused on the team. "Let's get moving then."

As the wagon started out once more, Mandie eased out a long breath, letting the tension flow from her chest with the spent air. All seemed to be well.

No sign of Clayton, and soon, she and Enoch would be preparing for their new life together.

CHAPTER 30

The sound of hammering from the sawmill echoed off the surrounding mountains as their wagon rolled into Walnut Springs, but Mandie barely heard it over the thundering of her own heart.

It was almost time.

Enoch reined in before the boarding house, and Robert emerged from the jailhouse down the street, his long stride carrying him to meet them.

"Good timing." Robert tipped his hat to Mandie and her mother. "Sheriff Hawkins is ready whenever you are. He suggested we hold the ceremony down by the cottonwoods near the river—says it's prettier than the jailhouse."

"That sounds lovely." Mandie glanced toward the river and the trees he must mean. A beautiful spot.

Enoch set the brake and swung down from the wagon, then moved to help Mandie and her mother from the rear bench.

His hands lingered at her waist as he lifted her down, and the warmth in his eyes made her breath catch. "You all right?"

She nodded, though her pulse quickened under his steady gaze. "Just ready."

"Me too." Was that a twinkle in his blue eyes?

She couldn't help a private smile.

Papa approached, brushing dust from his coat. "What about accommodations? You mentioned renting a room for the ladies?"

Robert gestured toward the boarding house with a grimace. "That's the trouble. Mrs. Patterson's full up with a group of surveyors passing through. But Mrs. Holbrook—" He nodded toward the mercantile across the street. "She's offered her own chamber above the store for Mandie to dress. Says it's the least she can do for such a special occasion."

"How kind of her." Mama's face brightened. "Though I do hope it's suitable…"

The creak and jingle of an approaching wagon drew their attention as Thomas arrived with Bea seated beside him on the driver's bench. Even from a distance, the older woman's face lit when she spotted their group.

"Bea!" Mandie called out, lifting her hand in greeting.

Thomas brought his wagon to a halt beside theirs, and Bea practically bounced with excitement as he helped her down. She hurried straight to Mandie, her wrinkled hands reaching out to grasp both of Mandie's.

"Oh, my dear girl." Bea's eyes sparkled. "What a wonderful day this is. Thomas told me everything on the ride—how you and Lord Enoch finally spoke your hearts to each other." She squeezed Mandie's hands. "I have been praying for this day since you first arrived at our ranch."

Warmth flooded Mandie's chest. "I'm so glad you're here. It wouldn't feel right without you."

Bea turned to clasp Mandie's mother's hands next. "You must be Mrs. Sinclair. I am Bea Wang. Your daughter has become very precious to all of us."

"Mrs. Wang." Mama's wide-eyed expression showed some

bewilderment at the housekeeper's easy warmth. "Thank you for caring for Mandie after her injury."

"Now then." Bea pulled back and clapped her hands together. "Let us get you dressed for this blessed occasion."

Within minutes, Mandie was settled in the Holbrooks' private chamber with her case and her mother and Bea. Mrs. Holbrook had graciously provided tea, as well as a pitcher of fresh water and clean towels. Despite the simple furnishings, the small room was cozy.

Her mother hung the ivory-trimmed dress from a peg on the wall, and Bea ran her fingers over the silk. "This is beautiful fabric. It reminds me of the dresses my mother wore."

Mama busied herself unpacking the small items they'd brought—a pearl necklace that had belonged to Mandie's grandmother, a pair of cream-colored gloves, and the ivory combs she'd worn at her first wedding.

"I thought perhaps we could arrange your hair differently this time." Mama lifted one of the combs. "Something softer, more suited to the setting."

Mandie nodded, settling onto the room's single chair as her mother moved behind her to begin working with her hair. Her fingers loosened the simple braid, then began brushing out the long waves. "Mrs. Wang, perhaps you could tell us about Enoch as a boy. Thomas mentioned you've been with the family since they lived in England."

Bea's face softened with memory. "Such a serious child, even then. He adored playing with Will, but he was always watching out for his younger brothers too. Always thinking three steps ahead." She began unfastening the tiny buttons that ran down the back of the dress. "But he had the sweetest laugh when something truly delighted him—a bubbling sound that would start in his chest and roll out until his whole face transformed."

Mandie couldn't help smiling at her mind's image of a young

Enoch with that same careful way of watching the world. "I can imagine that."

"He was always bringing me injured creatures." Bea shook out a wrinkle from the silk dress. "Baby birds, wounded rabbits, once even a fox kit with a broken leg. His mother would scold him for it, but Enoch never stopped trying to fix what was broken."

An ache settled in Mandie's chest. Or maybe a longing. She wanted to slip her hand in his and be at his side as he worked to make the world around him a better place.

"There." Mama stepped back to survey her handiwork. She'd swept Mandie's hair into a soft arrangement at the nape of her neck, with gentle waves framing her face. The ivory combs held the style without making it too formal. "Much better for an outdoor ceremony."

Over the next few minutes, they helped her into the elaborate gown, and she stood as her mother fastened the buttons, and Bea knelt to pull on her best slippers.

"There." Mama stepped back to examine her, a smile glistening in her eyes. "You look radiant."

Bea pushed to her feet, and a grin creased her face as she clasped her hands together. "Lord Enoch will be struck speechless when he sees you."

Mandie smoothed her hands over the silk skirt. She and Mama were of a similar size, so the dress fit perfectly, the ivory trim catching what light filtered through the small window. But more than the gown, a deep sense of rightness settled in her spirit.

"I should go tell the men you're ready." Bea moved toward the door, but she paused before slipping out. "Any messages to pass along?"

Mandie raised her brows as she scanned for something that might encourage Enoch. "Only that I'll be right behind you." She could say more when she was there in person and would see his response.

After Bea left, Mama fussed with the pearl necklace one final time, her fingers trembling as she adjusted the clasp. "Mandie. I want you to know how proud I am of the woman you've become. The strength you've shown these past months, the grace with which you've faced every challenge..." She paused, her voice thickening. "Your father and I, we didn't see past that man's charm, and I'm so very sorry."

Mandie turned to face her mother fully, reaching out to still those trembling hands. "Mama, Clayton showed you exactly what he wanted you to see. He's excellent at presenting a facade."

"But we should have protected you better. Should have listened when you tried to tell me you wanted nothing to do with him." Tears gathered in her mother's eyes. "Instead, I actually encouraged a connection between you. I thought it the perfect match since he was Nicholas's brother."

"And now look where the Lord has brought me." Mandie squeezed her mother's hands. "If I hadn't fled Savannah, I never would have found Enoch. I never would have discovered what real love feels like."

Her mother nodded, blinking back tears. "He does love you, doesn't he? I can see it in how he looks at you. How gentle he is with you."

"He does. And I love him more than I ever imagined possible."

Mama sniffed. "I suppose we'd better get you to him then."

They made their way down the narrow staircase to the mercantile's back door. Mrs. Holbrook waited at the bottom, beaming as they approached.

"Oh my dear, you look absolutely lovely." The older woman clasped her hands at her chin. "Sheriff Hawkins and the men are already down by the river. Such a romantic spot they've chosen."

"Thank you so much for the use of your room." Mandie took the woman's hands to squeeze them. "You've been a blessing."

"Happy I could help." Mrs. Holbrook's cheeks pinkened. "Now you go on and marry that handsome fellow. The whole town's been talking for years about how he needs a wife."

Mandie's mother opened the back door, and they stepped out into the warm afternoon air. The scent of pine and fresh air filled her lungs as they walked along the path behind the buildings, their footsteps muffled by the soft dirt.

The mercantile appeared to be connected to the building beside it, and perhaps one more, so they kept walking until a path between the structures would allow them to turn toward the main street and the river.

After they passed the second door, it opened behind them. Mandie glanced back, a smile and a pleasantry on her lips for the shop owner.

The man who exited looked nothing like a businessman. Nor the second who flanked him. But the third man…she knew far too well.

Clayton.

Before she could scream, one of the men lunged forward and clamped a grimy hand over her mouth as he dragged her backward, the stench of unwashed bodies and stale whiskey overwhelming her senses. She struggled against his grip, against the bitter taste of his palm against her skin.

Her mother's cry of alarm cut short as the second man seized her, dragging her backward toward the open door.

Mandie thrashed against her captor's hold, her silk skirt tangling around her legs.

"Hello, Mandie." Clayton's voice cut through the air, his words sending shivers down Mandie's spine. "No need for dramatics. We're simply going to have a conversation before you make any...permanent decisions."

She fought harder, and the ivory combs scattered from her hair, clattering onto the dirt as her carefully arranged waves tumbled loose.

The men dragged them into the dim interior of what appeared to be a storage room. Crates and barrels lined the walls, and the air reeked of old spices and something sour that made her stomach twist.

Clayton stepped inside, closing the door behind him. He turned the key in the lock, then pulled the key out and tucked it in his vest pocket. The dim light filtering from a single lantern cast his face in sharp shadows, making his smile appear even more predatory than usual.

"Much better." He brushed an imaginary speck of dust from his sleeve. "Now we can speak privately."

Mandie's heart hammered against her ribs. *Lord, please let Enoch come looking for us soon. Please don't let him wait long.*

Her mother whimpered behind the second man's hand, her eyes wide with terror above his grimy fingers. The sight sent fury blazing through Mandie's fear.

"Let her go," she tried to say, though the words came out muffled against her captor's palm. She bit down hard on the fleshy part of his hand.

The man cursed. "Little wildcat bit me!" But he clamped his grip tighter, covering most of her nose so she could barely draw air.

Panic surged up her chest. *Lord, we need help. Please!*

CHAPTER 31

$\mathcal{E}$noch stared at the front door of the mercantile, where Mandie should appear any second. What was taking so long? Bea had stepped through that entrance at least ten minutes ago, saying his bride and her mother would be right behind her.

"They're probably just having a moment." Bea rested a hand on his back, that motherly touch that should reassure him.

But it didn't. The coiling inside him only pulled tighter.

Mandie probably needed time with her mother. Time for the two of them to talk through all that had come between them. But something in his gut said this wasn't that moment.

He sucked in a breath and straightened. "I'm going to check on them." But as he stepped forward, his mind spun through what might hold them up. He turned back to his brothers and scanned them. "James, come with me?"

Just in case. No one had seen or heard of Clayton coming back through town, but that didn't mean the man wasn't lying in wait somewhere. Waiting to make his move.

And before Mandie married Enoch would surely be the moment he chose.

Now the tension in Enoch's gut surged up to create chaos in his mind. A flurry of images and possibilities for what the man could be doing to Mandie this very minute.

He broke into a run, sprinting the last section across the street up onto the boardwalk in front of the mercantile. He forced himself to slow so he didn't tear down the door as he burst inside.

Mrs. Holbrook jerked her head up from behind the counter, startled by their sudden entrance. "Mr. Balfour. Is everything all right?"

He heaved in air. "The ladies—Mandie and her mother. They haven't come down to the river yet." He fought to keep his voice level, though his pulse hammered against his collar. "Are they still upstairs?"

Mrs. Holbrook shook her head, confusion wrinkling her weathered features. "Oh no, they left through the back door maybe five minutes ago. Said they were heading straight to you."

Five minutes. His blood turned to ice. They should have reached the river before now.

"Which way did they go?" James stepped up beside him.

"Out the back, through the alley." Mrs. Holbrook started toward the rear of the store. "They were dressed so lovely, your bride especially. That gown with the ivory trim was just—"

Enoch wove between the shelves to follow her, James close behind him.

She led them through the narrow hallway to a door at the rear. She pushed open the door, and they stepped onto a dirt trail that ran behind the row of buildings.

"They went this way?" Enoch scanned the buildings connected to the mercantile, a single back door to each. No sign of ivory trim or Mandie's dark hair. No sign of anyone.

He started forward, scanning the ground and the buildings. The first door must be for the doctor's office. The next for the—

His gaze caught on something that stopped his breathing.

Ivory combs. Scattered in the dirt near the second building.

His chest constricted as he stooped to gather them. One was cracked, as if it had been dropped—or torn loose in a struggle.

"James." His voice came out rough as gravel. He held up the combs, and his brother's face went ashen.

"They were taken." James stepped closer to the second door, pressing his ear against the weathered wood. "This is the back of the saloon."

Enoch moved beside him, straining to listen.

At first, only silence. Then—muffled voices.

Men's voices.

Enoch held himself perfectly still, searching for words or tones that might sound familiar.

Then it came—a suave Southern drawl that made his blood heat to fire.

"Stay here and make sure they don't leave." He kept his voice to a whisper. "I'm going for help, then we'll go in through the front."

James nodded, then pulled aside his jacket to reveal a pistol tucked in the waistband of his trousers. Why hadn't Enoch thought to arm himself?

Because he'd come to his wedding, and strapped with a pistol didn't seem the right attire to greet his bride with.

He spun and charged down the alley to the nearest opening between the buildings. He needed the sheriff and his brothers from the river, then they could go through the saloon's front door to stop that madman.

When he emerged onto the street, he could see the others standing under the cottonwoods. He halted to yell, "Sheriff!"

Robert had already seen him though, and was striding toward him. Enoch waved for them all to come, and Sheriff Hawkins and his two brothers broke into a run. Even Mandie's father and Bea started toward him at a fast clip.

He turned toward the front of the saloon and waited just outside the door for the others. Better to enter with the sheriff than by himself.

As soon as the men reached him, Enoch spat out the details. "Clayton has them. We think they're being held in the back room of the saloon."

The sheriff's weathered face hardened. "You certain?"

"Found these in the alley." Enoch held up the broken ivory combs. "We heard Clayton's voice through the back door."

Hawkins nodded and turned to stare at the saloon door. Probably making a plan. "I don't think Nelson would have anything to do with this, but your man Clayton might have simply found a quiet spot to work from." He stepped forward and pushed the door open.

Enoch followed close, the others right behind him.

The dim interior reeked of stale beer and tobacco. Nelson, the owner, looked up from sweeping behind the bar, his bushy eyebrows rising at the sight of their group.

"Sheriff? What brings you—" The man's gaze took in their grim expressions and the way they all stayed grouped together. "Something wrong?"

Hawkins stepped closer. "Is there anyone else here? In the back?"

Nelson shook his head. "Will doesn't come until four. Why?"

Sheriff Hawkins rested an arm on the bar. "No one in your storage room?"

Nelson reared back as he frowned. "Shouldn't be. Why would you ask that?"

Hawkins eyed him. "We have reason to believe someone's holding two women in your back room against their will."

Nelson's brows shot up. "That's not possible. I keep that room locked." He reached into his vest pocket, then froze. He patted frantically at his vest, then his trouser pockets. "My keys...they're gone."

Enoch's jaw clenched.

"When did you last see them?" Hawkins straightened, pulling away from the bar.

"This morning when I opened up." Nelson's voice shook. He spun like he would charge down the hall to inspect the storeroom himself.

The sheriff raised a hand. "Hold up. We do this smart, or those ladies could get hurt."

Nelson paused and nodded.

The sheriff moved around the bar, keeping his voice low. "Is there another way into that room?"

Nelson shook his head. "Just the one door from the hallway. That last one before you go outside."

"James is watching the back of the building." Enoch's hands curled into fists. Every second they spent planning was another moment Mandie was trapped with that monster.

"Good." The sheriff turned to them all. "Here's what we'll do. Nelson, you stay here in the main room in case we need you. Mr. Sinclair, keep near the front door—make sure no one else comes in. The rest of us will move down that hallway, quiet as we can." He drew his sidearm, checking the cylinder.

"When we reach the door, I'll listen first. When I give the signal, we charge in. Fast and hard, so Clayton doesn't have time to hurt the women."

Enoch stepped forward. "Do you have a gun I can borrow? I didn't think I'd need one today."

Nelson reached behind the counter and pulled out a shotgun.

Enoch took it and nodded his thanks, then checked the chamber. Loaded and ready.

Every instinct screamed at him to charge down that hallway right now, but the sheriff was right. One wrong move could get Mandie killed.

His pulse hammered as they crept down the narrow hallway,

the floorboards creaking a little under their boots despite their efforts at stealth. The smell of old whiskey and dust grew stronger with each step.

At the back door, Enoch tried to let James inside, but the door was locked.

The sheriff positioned himself at the storage room door, pressing his ear against the wood. Enoch moved in to listen too.

Clayton's voice sounded inside, too low to make out words. Then a woman's muffled cry. Enoch's vision went red around the edges. That was Mandie's mother, he was almost certain.

Enoch pulled back when Hawkins did, and the sheriff held up three fingers in a countdown.

Enoch breathed in a steadying breath. *Help us, Lord. Protect the women.*

Two fingers.

He raised the shotgun and aimed.

One finger.

The sheriff lifted his boot and slammed it into the wood near the handle. The door exploded inward.

The small room erupted in chaos—shouts, a woman's scream, bodies pressed together in the cramped space.

Enoch surged in behind the sheriff, his eyes searching frantically through the dim light for Mandie. There—pressed against the far wall, held by a blighter with stringy hair and beard, her gown torn at the shoulder.

"Nobody move!" Sheriff Hawkins trained his pistol on Clayton.

But Clayton was already in motion, lunging toward Mandie with something glinting in his hand—a knife. "You'll not have her, Balfour!"

Enoch aimed the shotgun far enough away that stray buckshot couldn't hit Mandie, then pulled the trigger. The weapon bucked in his hands, the boom deafening in the cramped space.

Clayton spun sideways, clutching his belly, the blade clattering to the floor.

Enoch turned his gun on the goon who held Mandie, but the man was already releasing her. She surged away from the snake, nearly knocking him back into a stack of crates.

Mandie. Enoch held out an arm for her, keeping the shotgun steady in his other.

As she neared him, another gunshot cracked through the chaos—this one from Clayton's direction.

A woman screamed.

Enoch's insides nearly exploded. Had she been hit?

But Mandie closed the distance between them, crashing into his side.

The sheriff grunted and staggered, pressing his left arm against his middle, but he kept his weapon raised. "Drop it, Beaumont!"

Enoch wrapped Mandie tight with one arm. As much as he wanted to hold her, he had to get her out of danger.

He pressed his mouth near her ear. "Go out to the hallway till it's safe."

He had to almost shove her away from him, but at last she let go and slipped away.

He forced his full attention back to these kidnapping lizards.

Robert and Thomas had already pushed in around Enoch, and each had a stranger at the end of his gun barrel. The sheriff kept his weapon aimed at Clayton, and Mandie's mother stood curled into herself behind Robert.

Enoch motioned her out into the hall with Mandie while he kept his gun ready for any scoundrel who thought he might make a break for it.

At last, the women were safe. He glanced around for rope. Something to tie these men up.

"Nelson!" Sheriff Hawkins called toward the front of the

saloon, his voice strained but steady despite the bloody mark widening over his left shoulder. "Bring rope if you have it. And send someone for the doctor."

The saloon owner's footsteps pounded down the hallway, and within moments, he appeared with coils of rope and wide eyes as he took in the carnage.

"Help us tie them up." Enoch grabbed a section of the cord and stepped toward the stringy-haired man who'd held Mandie. The wretch didn't resist. He looked stunned by how quickly Clayton's plan had crumbled.

As he worked, Enoch eyed Clayton, who had slumped to the floor, his face ashen and his breathing labored. Blood seeped through his fingers where he clutched his middle, but his dark eyes still burned as they fixed on Enoch. "This…isn't…over."

"Yes, it is." Enoch's voice came out more of a snarl.

Robert and Thomas secured the second kidnapper while Enoch finished with the first, then moved to help the barkeep with Clayton. The sheriff, despite his wound, managed to keep his pistol steady on Clayton until they finished the job completely.

"Easy with him," Hawkins grunted as they hauled Clayton upright. "He's gut-shot, but I want him alive for trial."

As soon as the men were bound, Enoch slipped from the room to find Mandie. If they'd hurt her in any way…

She stood pressed against the hallway wall, her arms wrapped around herself. Her beautiful, dark hair spilled loose over her shoulders, and her gown hung torn at her neck, dirt streaking the silk, but she was whole.

Safe.

"Mandie." Her name came out rough, all the fear and fury of the past hour condensed into those two syllables.

She turned at his voice, and the relief that flooded her face nearly brought him to his knees.

In three strides, he reached her, gathering her into his arms with a desperation that shook him to his core.

"Are you hurt?" His hands moved over her shoulders, her arms, checking for injuries while his eyes searched her face. "Did they—"

"No." She pressed her face against his chest, her voice muffled but steady. "They didn't have time. You came so quickly."

He buried his face in her disheveled hair, breathing in the scent of her, grounding himself in the solid reality of her presence.

His bride. Safe in his arms, where she belonged.

Behind them, boots thumped, and he eased Mandie out of the way so his brothers and the sheriff could escort their prisoners toward the front of the saloon.

He couldn't bring himself to go with them. He couldn't leave the woman in his arms.

"Your mother?" He eased back just enough to search her face.

"Shaken, but unharmed."

Relief eased through him. He pressed his lips to her forehead, then pulled her tight. The last of the tension finally began to drain from his shoulders. "I thought I'd lost you." The words scraped raw from his throat. "When I saw those combs in the dirt..."

"I'm here." Her hands fisted in the back of his shirt, anchoring him to her. "I knew you'd come. I prayed you'd come quickly."

"I'll always come for you." Those words formed in his very core.

She nodded against his shirt. "What about our wedding? Can we get started with it soon?"

The question caught him off guard, and something like a

laugh escaped him. "You still want to get married today? After all this?"

She leaned back enough to send him the hint of a sassy smile. "If you're up for it. I want to be safely yours."

He was more than up for it. He pressed another kiss to her forehead. "Let's go see how the sheriff's feeling."

CHAPTER 32

The doctor's front parlor smelled of carbolic acid and lavender, a peculiar combination that somehow seemed fitting for this rather unusual wedding ceremony.

Sheriff Hawkins sat propped in a high-backed chair, his left arm secured against his side with bandages, but his weathered face bore a satisfied expression as he held a worn book in his good hand. The bullet had passed clean through his shoulder—painful but not life-threatening, unlike Clayton's wounds.

Buckshot to the belly at close range, Doc Hansen had muttered while tending to the sheriff's shoulder. *If that Beaumont fellow lives until the circuit judge arrives, it'll be a miracle. Course, won't matter much either way—kidnapping two women, rape, shooting an officer of the law. Sheriff's right that he's racked up enough offenses to hang.*

Enoch pushed thoughts of Clayton away as Mandie came to stand before him in the small parlor. Bea had managed to repair her gown, though a few stains darkened the ivory silk. Her rich brown hair had been re-pinned, with soft waves framing her exquisite face.

She looked radiant, despite everything they'd endured—

more beautiful than any woman alive. But then, Mandie had always possessed a strength that went deeper than surface appearances.

"Dearly beloved." Sheriff Hawkins's voice came strong despite his injuries. "We are gathered here in the sight of God to join this man and this woman in holy matrimony."

The familiar words washed over Enoch, and he drank in Mandie's face. Her warm brown eyes held his with such trust, such certainty, that something deep in his chest finally unclenched completely.

"Marriage is not to be entered into lightly," the sheriff continued, "but reverently, soberly, and in the love of God."

Love of God. Yes, that was exactly what this was—a gift he'd never expected, never thought he wanted again. Yet here stood the woman who'd shattered every wall he'd built around his heart, who'd shown him that love didn't have to mean loss. And if it did, the love would be worth the pain.

"Do you, Enoch Balfour, take this woman to be your lawfully wedded wife, to have and to hold, in sickness and in health, for richer or poorer, for better or worse, till death do you part?"

"I do." He put every ounce of certainty he possessed into the words. "Before God and these witnesses, I do."

Mandie's eyes shimmered, her lips curving in the softest smile he'd ever seen.

"And do you, Amanda Beaumont, take this man to be your lawfully wedded husband, to have and to hold, in sickness and in health, for richer or poorer, for better or worse, till death do you part?"

"I do." Her voice rang clear and true, without hesitation. "With all my heart, I do."

Sheriff Hawkins shifted in his chair, wincing as the movement pulled at his shoulder. "Then by the power vested in me by the Territory of Montana, I now pronounce you husband and wife." He looked up at Enoch with a knowing glint in his eyes. "You may kiss your bride."

Husband and wife. The words struck him like lightning, and for a heartbeat, Enoch simply stared at her—his wife.

His wife.

The reality of it crashed through him in waves, and his chest pressed in that familiar tightness. Yet this time it wasn't fear or the need to protect himself. It was overwhelming gratitude.

He cupped Mandie's face in his hands, his thumbs tracing the delicate line of her cheekbones as he searched her eyes. The complete trust there...the unwavering love...the joy that illuminated her from within... They all nearly undid him.

He lowered his mouth to brush her lips, his insides heating with the connection. This woman. He pulled back before the kiss could get out of hand. But he let himself linger in her eyes once more, taking her hands between his own.

"Lady Balfour." He couldn't help teasing her with the title.

Her eyes twinkled, as he'd suspected. "Lord Balfour."

Then the rest of the group was upon them, surrounding them with congratulations. Enoch gripped Mandie's hand as they faced their family. Soaked in the excitement. The well-wishes.

Through it all, she stood with him, holding his hand, slipping quiet looks his way. His insides warmed, and he gripped her hand tighter.

With this woman by his side and God in the center of their lives, the future that had once terrified him now beckoned with promise.

"No peeking." Enoch's voice held a note of barely contained excitement that made Mandie's pulse quicken as his warm hands guided her down the familiar hallway. The floorboards creaked beneath their feet, and she could smell the lingering scent of pine from the logs that formed the walls of their home.

"I can tell we're heading toward our room." She couldn't keep the curiosity from her voice, even as anticipation fluttered through her chest like moth wings. "You're being very mysterious, Lord Balfour."

"Patience, Lady Balfour." His breath warmed her ear, sending delicious shivers down her spine. "Trust me."

Trust. Such a simple word, yet one that had taken her months to truly embrace. Now it came as naturally as breathing when it came to this man—her husband of four weeks, though it felt both like a lifetime and mere moments since their wedding in Doc Hansen's parlor.

"Just a few more steps."

His hands remained steady on her shoulders as he directed her steps. She could sense the familiar dimensions of the hallway, could smell the beeswax Bea used to polish the wood floors, could hear the soft creak of floorboards beneath their feet. They were heading toward their room—the chamber that had been hers alone when she'd first arrived at the ranch, but which they now shared as husband and wife.

His former chamber sat empty save for the furniture he no longer needed. She'd grown accustomed to waking in his arms, to the steady rhythm of his breathing beside her in the darkness, to the way he'd rest his hand protectively over the growing swell of the babe each night.

Their child.

At seven months along, she could no longer hide the evidence of the life growing within her, and Enoch had made it abundantly clear that this babe was theirs in every way that mattered. He'd never once spoken of the circumstances of conception, never made her feel anything but cherished and protected.

His hands stilled her, and she felt him reach around her to push open a door. Not the door to their chamber, but the one to his former room. The hinges whispered softly as the door swung wide.

He guided her a few more steps, then stopped her again. "Open your eyes."

She blinked, her vision adjusting to the afternoon light streaming through the window. For a moment, she couldn't quite comprehend what she was seeing. There, positioned against the far wall, stood the most beautiful cradle she'd ever laid eyes on.

Her breath caught in her throat.

The wood gleamed with a warm honey patina, every curve and detail speaking of hours of careful craftsmanship. Smooth rails curved in graceful arcs, and delicate spindles had been turned with such precision they looked like fine lacework. The headboard bore a simple but elegant carving—a tree with spreading branches, its roots deep and strong.

"Enoch." His name came out as barely a whisper, her hand moving to cover her mouth as tears welled in her eyes.

"Do you like it?" There was uncertainty in his voice now, the confidence from moments before replaced by something almost vulnerable. "I've been working on it in the afternoons, in the barn. Wanted it to be perfect."

She moved forward on trembling legs, her fingers reaching out to trace the silken wood. The craftsmanship was exquisite—every joint seamless, every surface smooth as glass. She could imagine their child sleeping here, safe and warm in this cradle crafted by loving hands.

"It's perfect." The words came out thick with emotion as she ran her palm along the curved rail. "I can't believe you made this."

His arms came around her from behind, his large hands settling over the pronounced swell of her belly where their child grew. The babe responded immediately to his touch, rolling and stretching as if recognizing the familiar warmth of its father's hands.

"I wanted our child to have something that was made with love." His voice rumbled against her ear, low and steady. "Something that would last for generations. Maybe our grandchildren will sleep in this cradle someday."

The image his words painted—a future filled with children and grandchildren, a legacy built on the foundation of their love —made her chest tight with happiness. She leaned back against his solid chest, drawing strength from his presence.

"The tree." She traced the carved design with one finger. "What does it mean?"

His arms tightened around her, and he pressed a soft kiss to the sensitive spot just below her ear. "Family. Roots that run deep, branches that reach toward heaven. A place where everyone belongs and is loved for who they are." His voice carried a weight of meaning that made her heart swell. "I want that for our child—for all our children. A home where they know they're loved unconditionally."

The babe kicked again, a firm little foot or elbow pressing against her ribs, and Enoch chuckled. "Someone's awake in there."

"The baby always responds to your voice." Mandie covered his hands with hers. "Sometimes I think this little one loves you more than me."

"Impossible." His lips brushed against her temple. "But I'm grateful for every movement, every sign that our child is healthy and growing strong."

This man. How had she been blessed so very much?

Tears burned her eyes, along with the need to tell him what she'd never given voice to. It felt like he should know this new way he'd changed her life.

She took in a breath for strength. "I was afraid. When I first realized I was carrying a child. A child conceived the way…" She didn't need to finish, and the way Enoch's hands tightened around her, drawing her closer, soothing her spirit with his constant love, it gave her the courage to say the rest. "I worried I wouldn't be able to love the babe. Or maybe just simply wouldn't be a good mother."

"Mandie…" His voice came out almost in a groan, and he'd nearly wrapped himself around her now, as though his very closeness could prove her fears wouldn't come true.

She turned in his arms, needing to see his face, though the babe swelled between them. The late afternoon light streaming through the window caught the gold flecks in his blue eyes, and the pain there made her chest tighten. She pressed her hands flat on his shirt.

"God planted the love in my heart I feared I wouldn't have. And you showed me how to cherish someone when logic says it's not possible." She brushed her fingers over the stubble on his jaw. "With you doing this with me, I can't wait to see our babe. To learn how to be a good mother."

"Mandie." He cupped her face in his hands, his thumbs brushing away the tears that had spilled onto her cheeks. "You're going to be an extraordinary mother. I've seen how you care for others—how you've brought light and warmth to this house, how you've made Mrs. Wang smile more in the past months than I've seen in years."

She leaned into his touch, and she let her eyes close as she drew strength from his words. From his certainty. This man was such a gift.

"And as for the circumstances..." He paused, and she opened her eyes to meet his gaze. "That man gave us nothing but pain. But God—God gave us this child. This precious life growing inside you is a gift, Mandie. A blessing who will be raised with our love, not with what came before."

His words settled deep in her heart, filling the last hollow spaces where fear had lingered. She reached up to cover his hands with hers, holding them against her face as she absorbed the love in his voice.

How completely this man had claimed not just her heart, but their child's future as well.

A future that would be blessed indeed.

* * *

I pray you loved Enoch and Mandie's story!

James gets his story in the next book, and I think you'll love it even more!

* Mail-order bride
* Second-chance romance

* Boss/employee
* Class differences

Turn the page for a sneak peek of *Mail-Order Baroness,* book 2 in the Lords of the Rockies series!

By the way, would you like to read more about Two Stones and Heidi (the couple who Mandie rode with from Fort Benton to the Balfour Ranch)?

You can read their story in *Marrying the Mountain Man's Best Friend.*

SNEAK PEEK: MAIL-ORDER BARONESS

Chapter One

September, 1869

Balfour Ranch, near Walnut Springs, Montana Territory

"What's going on?" James Balfour propped his elbows on the polished oak table, glancing around at his three brothers as his insides knotted. They'd all gathered at Enoch's request, which meant something serious. Especially since he'd sent the women out of earshot, gone outside for a walk to see the horses pastured nearest the house.

Enoch leaned forward, voice low. "We need help." The words hung in the air like smoke from Mrs. Wang's kitchen fire.

James arched a brow, looking from one brother to the next. Enoch wasn't the sort to admit needing anything. "What kind of help?" Though he suspected the answer. He'd seen the fatigue in Mrs. Wang's face, the way she moved slower these days.

"For Mrs. Wang." Enoch's jaw worked. "She's kept this place running for years, never a word of complaint. But with

Mandie's condition…" He nodded toward the window, where his wife, very heavy with child, walked with their housekeeper. "And winter coming on early, it's too much for one person."

Enoch had a valid point. One James should have thought of himself.

Thomas, youngest of them all, spoke up. "She's not getting any younger. She's slower, even if she'd never say so."

The silence that followed felt final, as though they'd all known it and only now put it to words.

Robert nodded from across the table. "The preserving alone nearly did her in this year. All those vegetables from the garden, plus the meat from the cattle we slaughtered. She was up until near midnight for a week straight."

A familiar pang of guilt pressed in James's chest. He'd been so focused on the ranch work, on getting the cattle and horses ready for winter, that he hadn't paid enough attention to what was happening inside the house. Mrs. Wang had been like a favorite aunt—or maybe a mother—his entire life. He had to do a better job watching over her.

"So what are you thinking?" Robert settled back in his chair, arms crossed, gaze steady. "Hire someone from town?"

"That's the problem." Enoch ran a hand through his dark hair. "There's no one available in Walnut Springs. The few women who might be suitable are already spoken for or have their own families to tend."

"We could put out word farther south." Robert had that thoughtful expression he wore when his mind was calculating a problem. "Maybe someone in Helena would be willing to come up here."

James's mind began to race, an idea forming so suddenly it nearly took his breath away. Rose. Sweet Rose with her gentle hands and kind heart who used to help Mrs. Wang in the kitchen when they were children. Rose who'd disappeared from his life when he was eight, leaving nothing but an ache that had never quite healed.

Three pairs of eyes turned to James with varying degrees of surprise. Enoch's dark brows drew together. "Someone? Who?"

James cleared his throat, suddenly feeling like that eight-year-old boy again, trying to explain why Rose mattered so much. "Rose Prescott. You remember her—she and her mother came from England with us and lived here for a while before mum passed."

"Rose?" Enoch's face lit up with recognition. "Little Rose with the red hair who used to sing while she worked with Mrs. Wang?"

"That's her." Warmth spread through his chest at the memory. Her voice had such a soothing quality, he'd wanted to listen to it for hours. "She'd be perfect for this. She already knows the house, knows our family..."

"James." Enoch's voice carried a note of gentle warning. "That was fifteen years ago. She's not a child anymore, and from what I recall, she and her mother left rather suddenly."

"I know where she is." He spoke quietly, then immediately regretted the admission when all three brothers stared at him with renewed interest.

"You do?" Thomas leaned forward. "How?"

James shifted in his chair as heat crept up his neck. "Virginia City. She's...a singer there. Goes by Ruby Starling now. I saw an advertisement in the newspaper for her musical performances."

The hush stretched between them like a taut rope.

Robert spoke first, his gaze studying James, voice carefully neutral. "You've been keeping track of her."

It wasn't a question, and the weight of his brothers' scrutiny pressed in around him. "Not keeping track, exactly. Just...I heard about this singer, Ruby Starling, and something about the name struck me. Then I saw an advertisement in the Virginia City paper with a sketch of her." He paused, remembering the jolt of recognition when he'd seen that familiar smile staring back at him from the newsprint. "It was definitely her."

Enoch studied him with those piercing blue eyes that seemed to see straight through to a man's soul. "Virginia City's a rough place, James. If she's performing there..."

"She's making an honest living." He spoke more sharply than he'd intended. "Rose would never—" He caught himself. He sounded too defensive. "Look, I'm just saying she might welcome a change. Performing can't be easy work."

Thomas whistled low. "You want to bring a saloon singer up here to help Mrs. Wang?"

Heat flared through him. "She's not a saloon singer." And why did his brothers keeping insinuating she was? "Rose is a respectable woman who happens to have a beautiful voice. And she's family—or close enough."

Robert's brows lifted. "Even if she'd be willing to leave Virginia City, why would she want to come back here? If she's performing, she's probably making good money. Better than what we would pay for household help."

James's gut twisted at that very logical statement. Perhaps he could kick in more funds from his portion of the ranch proceeds. "Money isn't everything, Robert. Maybe she'd welcome the chance to be somewhere..." He paused, searching for the right words. "Somewhere she belongs."

"You're assuming a lot about what she wants," Enoch said quietly. "About what her life is like now."

The weight of truth in his brother's words settled like a load of rocks on his shoulders. He *was* assuming. He'd been assuming for years that Rose might want to hear from him, that she might miss what they'd all shared here before her mother took her away. The unanswered letters he'd sent through the years were proof enough of how wrong his assumptions could be.

"Besides," Thomas added, "if she's performing under a stage

name, she might not want her past following her. Some people leave for a reason."

James's clenched his jaw. "She didn't leave by choice. She was a child. Her mother made that decision."

"And now she's a grown woman who can make her own choices." Robert eyed him. "Including the choice not to return."

The logic was sound, but it did nothing to squelch the restless energy building in James's chest. He'd spent too many years wondering about Rose, too many nights staring at the stars and remembering the sound of her laughter echoing through these very rooms. What kind of life had Rose built for herself? Was she happy? Did she ever think of their childhood together, or had she put all of that behind her? Put him and his family out of her mind?

"Maybe she wouldn't," he said finally. "But it can't hurt to ask. The worst she can do is say no."

Enoch was silent for a long moment, his gaze fixed on something beyond the window. When he spoke, his tone was gentle. "If you want to reach out to her, James, you have my blessing. We'd all love to have Rose back if she's willing." He looked around the table at his other brothers, who nodded in agreement. "But don't get your hopes too high. People change. Circumstances change."

"I know." But even as he said it, a spark of hope kindled in his chest. Just the possibility of seeing Rose again, of hearing her songs fill these rooms once more, made something inside him come alive.

The scrape of chairs against the wood floor broke the stillness as his brothers pushed back from the table.

"Well then." Enoch stood and stretched his arms above his head. "I suppose we have our answer. At least a plan to try."

Thomas clapped James on the shoulder as he passed. "Good luck, brother. I hope she says yes."

Robert lingered a moment longer, his expression thoughtful.

"Just remember what Enoch said. Don't build this up too much in your mind."

James dipped his chin, though his pulse had already quickened with possibility. "I'll be careful."

While his brothers headed outside, he climbed the stairs to his room, his boots heavy on the wooden steps. The familiar creak of the seventh step, the way the afternoon light slanted through the hallway window—everything felt different now, charged with the potential of change.

His room faced west toward the mountains, and he stood at the window for a moment, watching the peaks catch the late afternoon sun. Somewhere beyond those mountains, Rose was living a life he knew nothing about. The thought both thrilled and unsettled him.

James settled at his small writing desk, pulling out a sheet of paper and his pen. But as the nib hovered over the blank page, doubt crept in.

How exactly did a man reach out to someone who'd been ignoring his letters for years?

The stark reality of those unanswered letters hit him like a cold mountain wind. Four letters over the years—carefully crafted, full of memories and updates on his family and gentle inquiries about her wellbeing. Four letters that had vanished into silence as complete as a winter snowfall.

If Rose wouldn't respond to James Balfour writing to her directly, perhaps she'd respond to someone else entirely.

A new idea began to form, one that made his chest tighten with both excitement and guilt. What if the letter didn't come from him at all?

The advertisement section of the Virginia City paper—he'd seen plenty of notices there for employment opportunities, respectable positions that drew responses from people seeking honest work.

He pulled out a fresh sheet of paper and dipped his pen in ink.

Seeking experienced woman for household management position.

He paused. Too formal. Rose would completely ignore that.

He marked through the words and started again.

Seeking Respectable Woman for Household Position

Household assistant needed for established Montana ranch family. Experience with cooking, cleaning, and general domestic duties helpful but not required. Suitable for woman seeking change from mining town life to peaceful mountain ranch.

Position includes room and board in comfortable accommodations, plus generous wages. Duties to include cooking assistance, general housekeeping, and companionship for female family members. Remote location requires commitment through winter months.

He studied the words, imagining Rose reading them in some Virginia City boarding house or theater. Would she be curious enough to respond? Would the promise of mountains and peace appeal to someone who'd been performing in the rough-and-tumble world of a mining town?

He added one more line: *Reply to Telegraph Office, Walnut Springs, Montana Territory.*

Would she think it odd for the correspondence to be held at the telegraph office? It was clear that he wanted to remain anonymous, but maybe that wasn't uncommon for general advertisements like this that might receive a horde of responses.

He glanced over the advertisement once more. This would do. He'd ride to town tomorrow morning to send the message to the Virginia City newspaper. That would be the *only* town he advertised in.

Then he'd give a week to wait for Rose's response. If she didn't answer, he'd ride to Virginia City himself and plead his case in person.

Certainly she couldn't resist a bit of the Balfour charm from her oldest friend.

He could only pray one of these steps would work. Something inside him had come to life with the thought of Rose back in his life, and he wouldn't give up this dream again. Not like he'd been forced to the first time she left.

<u>Get MAIL-ORDER BARONESS, book 2 in the Lords of the Rockies series, at your favorite retailer!</u>

Did you enjoy Enoch and Mandie's story? I hope so!
Would you take a quick minute to leave a review where you purchased the book?
It doesn't have to be long. Just a sentence or two telling what you liked about the story!

* * *

To receive a free book and get updates when new Misty M. Beller books release, go to https://mistymbeller.com/freebook

Brothers of Sapphire Ranch

Healing the Mountain Man's Heart

Marrying the Mountain Man's Best Friend

Protecting the Mountain Man's Treasure

Earning the Mountain Man's Trust

Winning the Mountain Man's Love

Pretending to be the Mountain Man's Wife

Guarding the Mountain Man's Secret

Saving the Mountain Man's Legacy

Sisters of the Rockies

Rocky Mountain Rendezvous

Rocky Mountain Promise

Rocky Mountain Journey

The Mountain Series

The Lady and the Mountain Man

The Lady and the Mountain Doctor

The Lady and the Mountain Fire

The Lady and the Mountain Promise

The Lady and the Mountain Call

This Treacherous Journey

This Wilderness Journey

This Freedom Journey (novella)

This Courageous Journey

This Homeward Journey

This Daring Journey

This Healing Journey

Call of the Rockies

Freedom in the Mountain Wind

Hope in the Mountain River

Light in the Mountain Sky

Courage in the Mountain Wilderness

Faith in the Mountain Valley

Honor in the Mountain Refuge

Peace in the Mountain Haven

Grace on the Mountain Trail

Calm in the Mountain Storm

Joy on the Mountain Peak

Brides of Laurent

A Warrior's Heart

A Healer's Promise

A Daughter's Courage

Hearts of Montana

Hope's Highest Mountain

Love's Mountain Quest

Faith's Mountain Home

Honor's Mountain Promise

Texas Rancher Trilogy

The Rancher Takes a Cook

The Ranger Takes a Bride

The Rancher Takes a Cowgirl

Wyoming Mountain Tales

A Pony Express Romance

A Rocky Mountain Romance

A Sweetwater River Romance

A Mountain Christmas Romance

www.ingramcontent.com/pod-product-compliance
Lightning Source LLC
Chambersburg PA
CBHW031034310726
48969CB00007B/1981